Mistletoe Memories

BERNADETTE MARIE

5 PRINCE PUBLISHING

Published by 5 PRINCE PUBLISHING & BOOKS, LLC

PO Box 865, Arvada, CO 80001

www.5PrinceBooks.com

ISBN digital: 978-1-63112-334-4

ISBN print: 978-1-63112-335-1

Cover Credit: Marianne Nowicki

4282023

THIS TITLE WAS ORIGINALLY PUBLISHED IN THE 2022 A CHRISTMAS TO REMEMBER ANTHOLOGY BY 5 PRINCE PUBLISHING

For Stan
I love you and I aways imagine mistletoe

Also by Bernadette Marie

THE KELLER FAMILY SERIES

The Executive's Decision

A Second Chance

Opposite Attraction

Center Stage

Lost and Found

Love Songs

Home Run

The Acceptance

The Merger

The Escape Clause

A Romance for Christmas

THE WALKER FAMILY SERIES

Walker Pride

Stargazing

Walker Bride

Wanderlust

Walker Revenge

Victory

Walker Spirit

Beginnings

Walker Defense

Masterpiece

At Last

THE ROM COM MOVIE CLUB

The Rom Com Movie Club - Book One

The Rom Com Movie Club - Book Two

The Rom Com Movie Club - Book Three

FUNERALS AND WEDDINGS SERIES

Something Lost

Something Discovered

Something Found

Something Forbidden

Something New

THE DEVEREAUX FAMILY SERIES

Kennedy Devereaux

Chase Devereaux

Max Devereaux

Paige Devereaux

STAND ALONE TITLES

The Happily Ever After Bookstore

Liz's Road Trip

THE MATCHMAKER SERIES

Matchmakers

Encore

Finding Hope

THE THREE MRS. MONROES TRILOGY

Amelia

Penelope

Vivian

THE ASPEN CREEK SERIES

First Kiss

Unexpected Admirer

On Thin Ice

Indomitable Spirit

THE DENVER BRIDE SERIES

Cart Before the Horse

Never Saw it Coming

Candy Kisses

ROMANTIC SUSPENSE

Chasing Shadows

PARANORMAL ROMANCES

The Tea Shop

The Last Goodbye

HOLIDAY FAVORITES

Corporate Christmas

Tropical Christmas

Date for Hire

Mistletoe Memories

CHAPTER 1

Five Years Ago

GRETCHEN

Cake baking week. I have had this week circled on my syllabus since the day I walked into the culinary school. This is the week where we bake cakes and decorate them. This is the week I'm going to shine.

Since the third grade, my side hustle has been selling cupcakes. My grandmother and I would make them every weekend when I was young. We elaborately decorated them, and gave most of them away, usually to the nursing home where my grandmother had many friends. But, every day, I'd pack two in my lunch. One was always for me, because I have a sweet tooth and my mother said I was born with it. The other cupcake was for the highest bidder.

The price of a cupcake in the elementary school cafeteria ranged from a quarter, on a really bad day, to a sticker that I really wanted, trade for line leader, or on the best day, Dillon Walker paid five dollars. I quickly realized that was all the money he had to his name, and he often went without lunch because he didn't have a lunch account and no one made him a lunch. I gave him the cupcake, and the five dollars back. From that day on, I brought three cupcakes a day. One for me. One for him. One for the highest bidder.

By the time I made it to high school, I was selling a dozen cupcakes out of my car a day. I never got in trouble for it. Some of the teachers were my best customers.

But now, among the students in class with me ready to learn the art of baking cakes, I will excel. This is my home turf. I did what I had to do to braise the meats and sauté the vegetables in the other lessons, but baking, this is where I will shine.

In a few years, I'll have my own bakery. Everyone will want a Gretchen Meyers cupcake or wedding cake. I will be the Vera Wang of wedding cakes, and the top bidders will be social elite.

I take my seat at the prep table on a hard metal stool. Of course I'm at the front of the room because I don't want to be overlooked when I wow everyone with my skills.

"Good morning," the words resonate through the open kitchen, only now filling with the other culinary students.

I look up from my notes to see the man who had wished us all a good morning, and my heart begins to hammer in my chest. God, if he wasn't the most handsome man I'd ever seen. Blond hair pulled back into a ponytail, and he has a dimple in his cheek when he smiles. He has a hint of stubble, and dark eyes that shimmer under the lights that illuminate his working space.

Before I have a chance to scan my gaze elsewhere, his eyes land on me, that smile widens, and that dimple gets deeper. Be still my heart.

"Hey," he says in a softer tone, since I'm close enough to hear it.

"Hey," I return because I seem to be stunned by him in some way. Men don't have this kind of effect on me, so what the heck?

He holds out his hand. "Levi Braddock."

I take his hand to shake it, but I know my mouth is hanging open. "Levi Braddock," I repeat.

He's laughing. "That's my name. What's yours?"

Oh, God! Levi Braddock is standing in my presence, holding my hand in his. This is only one of the biggest names in the industry here in Denver, and because I stalk his work, I know he's only twenty-seven-years-old and the most sought-after cake designer around. Rock stars, A-list actors and actresses, and politicians use him when they want a cake that no one will ever forget. He's royalty—my teacher—and my competition.

He once made a cake that mimicked the Denver skyline. It had been displayed at the Brown Palace Hotel, and I'd spent no less than three hours studying it and taking pictures. The man is a genius.

"Hello?" he says, still holding onto my hand.

"Gretchen," I blurt out my own name as if I just drank something bitter on my tongue. "Gretchen Meyers."

The smile is back, his hand is still gripped around mine. "It's very nice to meet you, Gretchen Meyers."

"Likewise."

Levi Braddock leans in over the table and examines my earrings. "Snowflakes? It's only October."

I touch my earring, as if to confirm that they're really there. "I like snowflakes."

"Snowflakes are nice, but why? It's not winter."

"They remind me that we all have talents, similar talents, but each one of us brings something unique to the table."

He nods slowly. "Everyone in here can make a cake, some of us just have a more unique talent for it?"

"Exactly," I confirm. "Unique like each snowflake."

"Well, Gretchen Meyers, I have a feeling we're going to learn a lot from one another."

CHAPTER 2

Present

GRETCHEN

There is going to be one winner, and that winner is going to be me. A ten-thousand-dollar cash prize, a sprinter van, and a contract with the Hermon's of Denver Hotel is all going to be mine. Not only does the winner take home the coveted winnings, and their cake will be displayed at the hotel, in the atrium which will be ornately decorated for the holidays. People travel from all over the world to see the display each year. The winner's cake—my cake—will be seen by millions in person and on social media.

This year's theme for the atrium will be Santa's Workshop, and there will be a life-sized replica made out of gingerbread.

From the moment I received the letter that said my bakery had been chosen as one of the participating bakeries in this year's competition, I've been brainstorming designs. I have notebooks filled with drawings and computer renderings of holiday themed cakes. The reindeer, with blinking red nose, so far is my thought, but it will be a massive undertaking.

The notebooks that litter my desk include ingredient lists to start making prototypes.

To be honest, it's hard to think about Christmas in July when your shoes melt to the asphalt. Therefore, I must have Christmas music playing through my earphones while I work.

The glory of Colorado weather is that it always breaks and gives you a change. However, we're on our fifth straight day of temperatures over one hundred, and Christmas just isn't on my mind, especially since we're turning out four hundred cupcakes for the grand opening of a new casino in Black Hawk this weekend. The ovens are going full time because we still have our normal business to attend to, and I look as if I've run a marathon. I feel as if I've run a marathon too. This year, wedding season trickled into July hard. My team and I have been cranking out wedding cakes, but that's where my passion lies, so I don't mind extra time put in to make a masterpiece for a bride, even though I'm uber-focused on cakes shaped like reindeer at the moment.

"I called on that flour delivery," Marsha, my manager and right hand, says as she walks into my tiny office at the back of the bakery, where the temperature is a balmy eighty according to the tiny thermometer I keep on my desk. "It'll be here Wednesday morning."

I rub the bridge of my nose because I knew her answer on the missing flour delivery wasn't going to be good news, and I was right.

"That's tomorrow," I point out. "But it puts our baking days behind."

Marsha shrugs. "What do you want me to do? I can call around, or we can wait it out."

I pull my bottom lip through my teeth. I want to tell this supplier to shove it, but I know it's not always their fault. Everything is hard to stock due to shortages, but I really want those cupcakes all done today. It would be one more thing to check off the list for this weekend.

The bell above the front door chimes and both Marsha and I look at the monitor on my desk which shows us the camera footage of the front end of the bakery.

"No way," Marsha drawls out the words.

"What is he doing here?" I say, looking at the image of the man in the chef coat, and long legs shrouded in black pants. My heart changes its rhythm, and I put my hand on my chest. I'm never sure if it kicks up because of how attracted I am to him, or if it thumps so hard in my chest because of how much I despise him.

"I guess you'd better go find out," Marsha whispers to me.

Standing up, I move toward her. My intention is to turn her and shove her out the door. "Nope, I pay you the big money, you go find out what he wants."

Marsha shakes her head. "You don't pay me that much money."

"I'm not going out there."

"Gretchen, it's your bakery and he's your ex."

CHAPTER 3

Present

GRETCHEN

I bite out a curse under my breath watching the cameras and realizing that Levi is walking through the bakery. A moment later he is standing in the doorway to my office, arm leaned on the jamb, a stern stare affixed on me.

"Can I have a minute?" he asks, and the gravel in his voice resonates in me as it always does—God, I hate that about him.

Marsha's eyes finally move from him to me. She's waiting for me to ask her to leave, but I don't want to be alone with him.

"Sure, what do you need?"

Levi walks fully into my office. "Marsha, would you mind giving us a moment alone?"

She hurries out, closing the door behind her. *Traitor*! I should fire her, but I can't. I need her. Instead, maybe I'll stab Levi with the scissors that are laying on top of my desk.

I actually wrap my hand around the handle of them, and he eyes me coolly, so I let go.

"What are you doing here?" I ask, and drop down into my office chair. It creaks beneath my weight because it lost a screw years ago, and I'm not going to replace it over one lost screw. I'm also not going to admit that I've gained a few pounds in the past few years. My grandmother would have attributed that to happiness in what I'm doing. But then again, she'd always been kind when it came to my weight and was a huge advocate in me loving my body at any size.

"I need a favor," he says, scanning a look over me.

That alone should have me grabbing for those scissors again, but Levi has never looked at me and not shown appreciation for what I look like. Even covered in flour, my hair piled on top of my head, when his gaze lands on me, there is a sparkle in his eyes. Damn him!

"I think your days of asking me favors and getting them are long over," I say, drawing his attention back to my eyes.

Levi leans his long body against my desk, his hand resting atop the stack of purchase orders I have laying there. "This is business, not personal."

"With you, business is personal. I don't plan to mix either."

Picking up a gold-plated pen from the top of my desk, Levi rolls it between his fingers. "You're going to hate me forever?"

"And a day if I can," I promise.

"Then I might as well tell you what I need."

I raise a brow and wait.

Levi looks at the pen, reads the inscription, and lays it back on the pile of papers. "I need flour. You always over buy, so I know you can help me out."

I curl up the side of my mouth and scan a look over him. His chef's coat has the name of his bakery on the chest—and what a chest.

He swims. It's how he blows off steam and keeps in shape. Another thing I despise about him, I consider.

I move my gaze upward to his face—and what a face. His eyes are dark and warm, and a stark contrast to the blond hair that's short and always a bit mussed from his fingers. I've never been able to decide if I like the shorter hair or his ponytail of years ago. He wears both so well.

I wince at the thought.

I shouldn't care what his hair looks like. I don't have to care for him at all, I have to remind myself.

Levi's lips part, as if he's going to say something, but I hold up my finger.

"I happen to have an enormous order going out this weekend, and I'm fresh out of flour. In fact, I'm waiting on an order myself."

He cocks a brow. "An enormous order?"

"Gigantic."

"Would it be cupcakes for a casino?" he asks, and I feel my jaw tighten.

"What I'm doing is none of your—"

"I'm making four hundred cupcakes for *Press Your Luck Casino*," he admits. "So is *Charlotte's Goodies*."

I press my hands to my thighs because they've begun to shake. "Seriously?"

Levi shrugs. "I guess they figured they'd hedge their bets in case one of us fell through. Then again, they do this to us every year."

"I could have easily delivered them twelve hundred cupcakes, and so could you."

"I'm not judging their business model. I'm taking the business. But I'm taking on a lot of business, and right now I'm out of flour."

I picked up the pen that Levi had examined when he'd

leaned against my desk earlier. "I'm not getting my delivery until tomorrow. I just can't—"

"You can."

"I don't want to."

He curled his lips into a tight little smile that makes his eyes sparkle, and I know he does that because he knows how sexy I think it is when that dimple in his cheek pops.

"You do want to. Not because you want to help me, but because you don't want me to fail and not show up. You want to see if I can show up with something even as close to perfection as yours."

I really hate him. "I'd love nothing more than to see your team pull up to unload, and all of the trays slide out of the back of your van."

"That's what I thought," he said smiling wider. "All I need is two bags."

I tilt my head to the side. "You came here for two bags? You could go to Costco for—"

"I did. They don't have any either. Neither does the restaurant store or the six suppliers who I called. Everything in town is headed here tomorrow."

With that bit of knowledge, I knew he wouldn't be the only one dropping by then.

"Then it appears I'm the only bakery in town who can fulfill these orders."

Levi puckers his lips and keeps his eyes fixed on me. "I guess that's that."

"I guess so," I said and wait for him to leave, but he doesn't. Instead, he reaches his hand out to a curl that refuses to tuck into my ponytail, and he wraps his finger into it.

I don't care how much the closeness of him makes my body temperature rise, or how much looking into those eyes makes me want to wrap myself around him, I can't stand him, and there is no way I'm going to help him.

CHAPTER 4

Five Years Ago

LEVI

I can't decide if the cake I'm looking at is a masterpiece or an abomination, according to the look on the face of the woman who decorated it.

After Gretchen completed culinary school, she was immediately approached by a local bakery to design wedding cakes. She'd been ecstatic to get the offer so quickly, and she'd taken it without asking me what I thought. Admittedly, that was a bit upsetting, since I'd wanted to snatch her right out of the school for my own bakery as an apprentice.

But I'd missed my chance, and she'd been so proud of herself, I hadn't told her of my plans.

In time she'll come to work for me. She has too much talent not to work for me, since I have the most sought-after bakery in Denver.

"It's gorgeous," I say, taking in the detail of the multi-tiered cake.

"It's gaudy," she laughs and the sound of it perks up every

nerve in my body. She's had that effect on me since the day I introduced myself to her at the school—as her teacher.

"It's exactly what the couple wants," I remind her.

"It's exactly what the *bride-zilla* wants. I'm scared for her to see it."

She's chewing on the side of her thumb, which she does when she's nervous.

I reach for her hand and ease it from her mouth, keeping it in my hand. We both stare at the cake.

It's a four-tiered cake in multiple colors. It has pillars that are shaped like crayons, and the icing drips down the tiers as if the crayons had been melted over the cake.

We each tip our heads from side to side.

I purse my lips, having decorated my share of strange-themed cakes. "Kindergarten teacher?" I ask.

Gretchen turns and looks at me. The line between her brows is deep. "Office supply store manager, marrying the owner of the store."

"Hmm," I say, her hand still clasped in mine. "To each their own."

"This isn't really what I thought I'd be doing when I took the job," she whispers. "I want to build creative cakes that people are afraid to cut into. Cakes so unique that they're put on display."

The woman she's working for isn't going to sell cakes quite like Gretchen wants to design, but at least the drive is still in her. When she's ready, I'll scoop her up, and she'll be ready to create the masterpieces she wants.

"Well, it's beautiful, for what it is," I say. "You did an amazing job."

She does this little body wiggle thing when she's proud of herself. It's a mix between a dance and a strange little shimmy. It's cute as hell.

She gives my hand a squeeze, since I haven't let go of her yet. "Let me get cleaned up and we can go."

Gretchen moves and because I don't let go of her hand, it tugs her back. She looks up at me.

"It's a great cake. I mean it," I say.

She bites down on her bottom lip, pulling it through her teeth, and then the smile breaks through. "Thank you. You taught me everything you know," she teases and moves from me.

I watch as she cleans up her workspace and stores the cake. If Charlotte knew I was standing in her bakery, Gretchen would be fired on the spot.

It's worth taking the risk on nights she works late just to watch her create. I have an enormous staff of talented people I've trained, but Gretchen outshines them all. In fact, I worry, that in time, she'll be better than I am.

There's room for everyone in this industry, I have to often remind myself. And like she once explained about the snowflake, when I met her, each of us has a unique talent. Gretchen's is just most unique.

But if we ever stopped being friends, I have no doubt she could win over all of my clients.

She appears again, hiking her purse up onto her shoulder, having removed her chef coat. Her hair is still pulled up, but she looks fresh walking away from having slaved and fretted over that cake.

She's taken off her leggings, and now looks evening-ready in the dress she had on under her chef coat. I know her well enough to know that the work shoes will come off in the car, and in her bag will be a pair of cute sandals. She's not one for heels, but she always has bright toenails she loves to show off even in December.

I've more than once scolded her for how she dresses in the winter, but she says she's always hot. Besides, she's told me,

I'm the only one she dresses up for, so I suppose I'll enjoy her frozen toes and cold knees that she exposes when she dresses up.

"Where are you taking me?" she asks as we shrug on our coats and walk out of the bakery. She turns and locks the door behind us.

"Soft opening," is all I say, and she knows that I mean to a new restaurant. We attend openings often, especially when former students invite me.

As she puts her keys back into her bag, I laugh, and that causes her to look up at me.

"What's funny?" she asks, and I point up to the entrance of the bakery.

Above the door is a sprig of mistletoe.

Her cheeks pink, though I don't know if that's because of the mistletoe or the cold.

"I wonder who put that there," she says with her voice shaking.

"You know, you can't just walk under mistletoe and not kiss."

Her eyes go wide. "We don't kiss."

I shrug. "Friends can kiss."

"You want to kiss me?"

"It's just a kiss, Gretch. Besides, what if its bad luck not to kiss?"

Her brows draw inward. "Bad luck?"

I shrug again. "We'd better just do it."

She laughs and rises on her toes. "Fine. Kiss me."

Wrapping my arms around her, I pull her into me hard, and she lets out a grunt and then a laugh. Something sparks in that moment. Something I'd never felt before. Tilting my head, I press a kiss to her lips and let it linger for only a moment.

Slowly she lets out a breath into the cold air as she eases

back. "Okay, then," she says, pressing her fingers to her lips. "We've warded off bad luck."

"I guess we have."

She loops her arm through mine and moves in close to ward off the cold as we begin to walk, perhaps moving as to not face whatever passed through us. "So, fancy food or good food?" she asks, redirecting our conversation back to the one before the kiss.

I laugh. Gretchen is a foodie, which most of us in the culinary industry are, but she loves a good meal, and one that's not too pretentious.

"I suppose we'll have to see." I cover her hand that holds my arm with my hand. Having her close to me, even if not in my bakery, keeps me sane.

CHAPTER 5

Present

LEVI

At least my bakery has better air flow than Gretchen's. I'm not sure how she manages day to day during the summer when the temperatures swelter as they have been.

I walk through the back door of my bakery, and the kitchen is bustling. My manager, Aerial, is looking over the cupcake order for the casino. The order is due on Saturday morning, so they'll be frosted Friday night. For now, they're cooling.

"Did you get the flour?" she asks optimistically.

I hold out my empty hands and she curls her upper lip.

"She wouldn't give you any?"

"She will," I say. "She'll always take care of me."

Aerial's eyes narrow. "That makes you sound chauvinistic."

I shrug. "I just know how she really feels."

"She hates you."

"She says she does. But deep down inside she loves me."

Aerial coughs out a laugh and looks back down at the clipboard in her hand. "She did love you, once. I've seen her around you. I don't think she feels that way anymore."

"Well, my comment still stands."

I look at the cake on the table that Aerial had been working on.

"Lancaster wedding?" I ask, ending one conversation and starting another.

"Groom's cake is finished. Janine is finishing the flowers for the wedding cake."

I nod. "Did my statues arrived for the Carter wedding cake?"

Aerial grins. "Sitting next to your workstation. They're hideous."

"Love is a strange thing. Some people want cherubs, some people want decapitated statues and blood red cake."

Her body shakes as if the whole thing creeps her out, which I know it does. "Why did you take that job?"

"They're paying top dollar for my expertise," I say as I walk back toward my workstation.

The design portfolio for the headless statue cake is on the top of the pile. Another ornate cake, a Ferrari, is the next design I'll tackle.

I move the papers until I come to my design for the Hermon's of Denver Hotel contest.

This year it's my bakery against Gretchen's and Charlotte's. Deep down I feel as if someone set this up. The three of us have always competed. Charlotte had been the number one bakery in Denver until I started up my own. I'm good at what I do, but I know luck played into that a bit. I designed the right cake at the right time, and the media exposure was phenomenal. Of course, my past relationships from Chicago helped to fuel my popularity. From then on, it was as if I had celebrity status and her bakery suffered.

When Charlotte hired Gretchen right out of culinary school, I knew it was to keep me from hiring her. Charlotte and I have years of experience over Gretchen, but standing alone at my work counter, I can admit, to myself, no one is better than Gretchen.

I study my design for the contest. It's a sparkly snowman with a top hat and winter boots. After the bakery closes at night, I've been working on the fondant to get the right amount of sparkle to it. It would appear to be a simple design to the untrained eye, but I know it will be amazing. In fact, I know it's good enough to beat Charlotte. My only true competition is Gretchen.

Wednesday evening, I settle down at my design table after the bakery closes and everyone has gone home. No one is home waiting for me—no one cares that I'll be sitting at this table until midnight. That, I suppose is the life of a single entrepreneur.

I have my pot of coffee brewed, and I'm sipping my first cup of the evening when I hear the knock at the back door.

Tap! Tap, tap-tap! Pause. *Tap! Tap, tap-tap!*

She might hate me, but Gretchen is predictable.

She's used that same knock since I met her. I stand from my stool and walk to the back door, opening it without even looking out into the alley to see who it is.

At my feet are two enormous bags of flour, and Gretchen is walking back toward her car.

"Oh, no," I call after her. "You don't just get to dump these at my door like a goodwill deed and walk away."

She stops, her keys held tightly in her hand, and looks at me. Standing just beyond the back bumper of her car, I take in the sight of her in a pair of shorts and a tank top. The softness of her always sends my body into a confusing whirlwind of emotions.

Just as it had been the day before, her hair is a mess piled atop her head, and she never wears makeup unless she's going out. I've always loved that about her.

"You needed flour. I had two bags extra."

Crossing my arms in front of me, I lean against the door-jamb. "And you're feeling generous?"

"I'll take them back if—"

"No. No, I need them."

"Okay then." She brushes a strand of hair from her forehead and tucks it behind her ear, which is pierced four times and always adorned with little gold hoops, except on special occasions when she wears snowflakes. "I'll send you a bill."

"Why don't you come in and I'll just give you the money."

"That's okay, I'll—"

"Gretch, just get in here," I say before I turn around and go back into the bakery, leaving her in the alley.

From my office door, I can hear the sound of her arming her car.

"You can't just leave those at the back door," she calls out.

"I won't. Come in here."

It takes her a full minute to appear in my office door, which means she stood there contemplating the move before she made it.

"How much?"

Her eyes go wide. "I didn't look."

I can't help but smile now. I knew she'd help me out. She might hate me, but nah, she doesn't.

"You just dropped them off without knowing how much you want for them? They're a hot commodity, you could spike up the price and sell them around town."

Those wide eyes flashed the truth of my statement. And because she didn't come with a price in mind, that means she came to see me. She'll never admit it, but I know her well enough.

"I'll bill you."

"I'll pay you over what my last invoice price was."

Gretchen quickly nods. "That's fine."

I pull my checkbook out of my desk drawer and begin to write the check.

"Aren't you going to look at an invoice?" she asks.

"I already did. I was sure you'd show up here with the bags."

Her hands fly upward, and she turns around and heads toward the backdoor. Curses are shouted, and I shouldn't laugh, but I can't help it.

If she's going to hate me, then I'm going to push her buttons.

I tear the check out of the book and make it to her car before she climbs into the driver's side.

"I added a delivery fee to it too," I say.

Gretchen rips the check from my hand. "I didn't have to help you."

"No, you didn't. I owe you one."

"Just forget it," she spits out the words as she climbs into her car, but I move my body in between the car and the door so she can't shut it.

"I was hoping that when you stopped by I could show you my Christmas design."

She narrows those blue eyes on me, and her lips go thin. "You want to show me, your competition, your Christmas design? For the hotel competition?"

I nod.

Gretchen shakes her head and reaches for the door, though she can't shut it with me standing there.

"You're full of it. Just as you always have been," she growls. "You just want to show me what you're planning so I'll tell you what I'm planning. It's not going to work. You're not going to screw me over again."

When she says things like that, it stings. But, yeah, she has every right to be mad at me. Though, I think it should have run its course by now.

I step back. "Thank you for the bail out," I say.

"It'll never happen again."

CHAPTER 6

Present

GRETCHEN

The man infuriates me. Looking in my review mirror, I can see him still standing in the alley watching me. His arms are crossed in front of him, and his grin, that stupid grin, on his mouth.

Why did I bother to do this for him? What do I owe him?

Nothing. I owe him nothing.

I turn out of the alley and head toward home. Now I'm mad at myself, so I dip my hand into the share size bag of M&Ms and take a handful. Popping the entire take into my mouth, I sit without chewing for a moment. I'm drowning my irritation in chocolate, which is a horrible habit, but other people would do it with alcohol, and that seems to be perfectly acceptable.

Regardless, I did what I did, and it didn't turn out any better than I thought it would. A moment in his presence just confuses me and makes me think about years ago when he was all I could think about. Now I have my business and that's all that matters. I need to keep my focus, now that I know he's working on his design, which undoubtedly will be a masterpiece.

Mine will be too, I assure myself, swallowing down the chocolate that has melted against my tongue. I'm good at what I do. I'm now the one that makes designer wedding cakes for celebrities, just as I'd always dreamed of doing.

Traffic is jammed at the end of the street, forcing me to turn right. I grip the steering wheel, because this will take me right in front of Levi's bakery.

I've been in there a thousand times, there's no need for me to turn my head to look at his window display, but I can't stop myself.

I never could.

As always, some elegant cake creation spins on a pedestal in the front window. Even though the store is closed for the night, the front window will be illuminated.

I can't help but look as I pass. How many hours of my life have I spent standing in front of that window? Once upon a time it was to be inspired. Then it was helping with the display when he was short-staffed or it was late at night. Now, I try very hard to look the other way if I end up on that street.

But as usual, I can't help but look at the window.

A six-tiered, multicolored cake spins in the beautiful display. Pots on each side of the cake collect the bounty from the rainbow slide that circles the cake.

I hate how talented that jerk is. And though his team helps build his masterpieces, he's behind every one of them.

I turn my head back to the road and slam on my brakes. My gawking at the store almost has me rear-ending the car in front of me.

Taking in a breath, I try to will my racing heart to calm down. Then I look in the rearview mirror, and the guy in the delivery truck behind me is staring at the window too. He's going much too fast and doesn't slow. A moment later he slams into the back of my car.

The first voice I hear when I open my eyes is Levi's. He's standing at my side, but I'm still buckled in my seat.

"Gretchen. C'mon, baby, talk to me," he says.

"Go away," I say, my head throbbing and my chest aching.

I can hear him chuckle, though he's blurry when I try to look at him. "There she is. Don't move. I don't want you to move until the paramedics check you out."

"I'm fine."

"You're dazed."

"You're not a doctor," I argue.

"No, and you've never been a good patient. So just sit still until they get here."

As I sit there, still buckled in my seat with Levi at my side, the shock begins to wear off, and my body begins to ache. The car is full of dust, and Levi has the towel that was tucked into to his apron pressed to my head.

The airbags had deployed. That S.O.B. hit me harder than I thought, and I hit the car in front of me.

There is a sharp pain in my shoulder that has me sucking in a breath.

"Unbuckle my seatbelt," I tell him, but he shakes his head.

"No. Let them do that."

"I'm not going to escape," I try to yell at him, but it takes too much breath to be loud. Besides, his face is nearly pressed up against mine with the towel.

He's still shaking his head. "When they know it's safe for you to move even the slightest bit, they'll take it off you. Please just do me this favor and sit still," he says, his voice soft and calm, which is just like him in a hectic situation.

"I'm done doing you favors," I manage.

"So you said. But do me one more."

I have no idea how long I've been here with him watching me, sopping up blood from my head.

It feels as if it's been forever, but I'd like to think that the local fire department and the paramedics will be quick to respond.

It's a woman who begins to talk to me next, inching Levi out of the way, holding the towel and unbuckling my seatbelt. She asks me questions that are so obvious, but it takes me a few moments to come up with all the answers. She shines a light in my eyes and pokes at me in different places.

"We're going to have the ambulance take you to the hospital to look you over," she says waving at someone.

"I'm fine. Can I just get a ride home?"

She smiles at me, her face finally sharper and not with the same cloudy haze it had a moment ago.

"You were hit pretty hard from behind. It would be better if you were seen at the hospital. Besides, the airbag clocked you right above the eye. You'll need some stitches."

Just hearing the word stitches makes me woozy.

"What about my car?" I ask.

I'm panicking now. I'm too busy to be without my car. I deliver in it. I meet clients with it.

Clients. I have a meeting tomorrow with the daughter of one of the coaches of our NFL team. I can't miss that. It will be one of the biggest weddings of the year, and she asked for me to design her cake.

"Gretch, I'll get everything out of your car and bring it to you," Levi says as the woman steps back and lets him in.

"Can't you just bring me my car? I'll need to drive home from the hospital."

A line forms between his brows as it does when he's concentrating hard, or is concerned.

"Honey, your car is totaled. It's not going anywhere."

His face is fuzzy again. "I need my car. It's part of my business. I have a meeting tomorrow."

"I don't think you do." He brushes my hair from my face and tucks it behind my ear. "I'll get everything out of your car and meet you at the hospital."

People start moving between me and the door to the car. Levi is pushed out of the way, as they begin to gingerly assess me. Putting a collar on my neck as they lift me from my seat. They're being extra careful of my shoulder, and it aches so bad that I think I might just pass out.

I get my first look at my car when they get me on the gurney and push me toward the ambulance. That jerk totaled my car!

Levi appears at my side again. "I pulled your purse out of your car. I gave them all your information, and I'll follow you to the hospital."

Seeing what my car looks like has put a panic in my chest that's making it hard to breathe. Am I hurt worse than just the ache in my shoulder?

"Okay," seems to be all that I can say.

"Marsha is headed over here. She's going to make sure they get your car towed off, and she's going to take everything with her from inside."

Tears are burning my eyes. "Thank you."

The smile that forms on his mouth says I'm a mess, because I just thanked him.

"I'll be there as soon as I can."

"Promise?"

"I do," he says, taking my hand and giving it a squeeze as they lift me into the back of the ambulance.

CHAPTER 7

Present

LEVI

The ambulance pulls away without sirens, and I know that's a good sign, but deep inside, I want them to get her to the hospital as quickly as possible and fix her. To look at Gretchen, she looks fine, but she's dazed. The paramedic said her shoulder might be dislocated too. And of course, the gash on her forehead is going to need stitches.

Steadying myself, I lean up against the light pole outside my bakery and run my fingers through my hair reminding myself to breathe, while gripping Gretchen's purse in my other hand.

"Levi! Levi!" Marsha's voice rings out over the chaos still in the street. "Where is she? What happened?"

She's at me before I can fully get my balance standing upright. It's then I notice they're finally getting the man out of the truck that hit Gretchen. He's worse off than she was. Her car took most of the impact, but he obviously didn't have a seatbelt on, and his face is bloody.

Marsha grabs hold of my arms and shakes me. "What happened. I thought she just got rear ended. Where is she? Her car is totaled."

I manage to pull her toward the front door of my bakery where we are away from the chaos, only slightly.

"They took her to the hospital to check her out. She's a little foggy, she needs stitches, and her shoulder might be dislocated."

Marsha's eyes went wide. "She can't be hurt."

"I'm going to the hospital now. I told her you'd get everything out of her car and take it with you."

Her brows draw inward. "You're going to the hospital? Maybe I should go. I'd hate for her to have a heart attack when she saw you."

"She's seen me. We're okay."

One of Marsha's brows rises now. "She brought you that flour, didn't she?" I don't answer and a smile curls up the corner of Marsha's mouth. "She hates you."

I can't help but smile either. "I know she does. She has every right to."

Marsha turns around and looks at Gretchen's car. "This isn't good. We have to get the cupcakes to the casino. She has a meeting tomorrow with Olive Darling. This isn't good."

My ears perk up at the name. "Gretchen is meeting with the Darlings?"

When Marsha's eyes refocus on me, they're angry. It's not much different to how Gretchen looks at me.

"Don't you go trying to take over that appointment," she threatens. "Gretchen has worked too hard on landing this wedding."

"I wouldn't do that." Heck, even if I did, Olive Darling hates me more than Gretchen does.

Marsha's lips pucker. "I know there's a reason she hates you, so I don't know if I can trust that."

What else can I say? Gretchen has obviously shared her feelings about me with her team.

"I can be trusted," I assured her, gripping Gretchen's purse in my hand. "I'll have her call you as soon as they allow it," I say, realizing her phone might still be in the car.

"I'm going to hold you to that."

I nod, then move past Marsha to Gretchen's car as the ambulance drives away with the driver of the truck.

Her phone is on the floor of the passenger side. I pull open the door, pick up the phone, and notice that in the cup holder is the snowflake ring from the top of a cupcake I'd given her years ago. I pick it up and study it.

It's faded considerably, but she always kept it in her car. But after all these years, I wonder why she still does. I can't help but grin. Maybe she doesn't hate me as much as she says she does. I tuck the ring in my pocket, and head back to my bakery with her purse and phone.

I weave my way through the emergency room to the curtained off area following the nurse. I hate hospitals, and it's then I decide I should have let Marsha come in my place. Not only do hospitals make me jumpy, but Gretchen isn't going to want to see me.

"She's in here," the nurse says, pulling back the curtain.

"Thank you," I say as I step into the tiny space where Gretchen sits upright on a bed. "How are you feeling?" I ask, and then notice her eyes are filled with tears, and she favors her left arm in front of her.

"I'm screwed," she says on a sob, then lifts her fingers to the bandage above her brow.

I move in beside her, on the side she isn't favoring. I sit down on the bed, facing her, and she eases against me, resting her head against my chest.

I soothe my hand over her hair, just as I would have done years ago, and in that moment it all feels right.

"Your shoulder?" I ask.

"They put it back in place, but there's a torn muscle," she sobs. "I have to have it in a sling for a few weeks."

I still my hand at the base of her neck and press my cheek to the top of her head. "You have a first-class team who isn't going to miss a step, it's all going to be okay."

"No," she says, easing back and wiping her cheeks with her free hand. "I can't be down like this. I have the cupcakes for the casino to deliver. I have to start working on the Christmas display. I have a meeting tomorrow with..." she stops talking and her eyes go wide.

"I know who you're meeting with tomorrow. It's okay."

"Marsha told you, didn't she?"

"I don't think she meant to."

Gretchen eases back against the bed and the need to touch her has me lifting my hand to her cheek. "She doesn't know who I am. I mean, in relation to you."

"There's no reason she ever would. My life with Olive was a long time ago, and in Chicago. I wouldn't have thought she'd follow her father to Denver." I brush my thumb over her cheek. "When she sees what you can do, you'll be her only choice."

"At least you can't steal the job from me, right?" She chuckles, but her eyes flash dark.

I ease back. I don't know if she meant for the words to hurt, but they slice through me. Wiping my hand over my mouth, I watch her. No, I don't think the words were meant to hurt me. The way her lip twitches, it appears that the words hurt her too.

"Gretchen?" Marsha's voice draws both of our attention to the door. Her eyes are wide, and I don't know if it's because of how close Gretchen and I are sitting, or how pale Gretchen looks now that the bruise on the side of her forehead is starting to darken. She must have hit her head on the door window too.

Marsha moves to the side of the bed, and I stand.

"You should come on this side. She dislocated her shoulder and has some muscle tears," I tell Marsha.

She nods and moves around the bed and past me to take my place on the edge of the bed.

As I back away from the bed, Marsha is already peppering Gretchen with questions. No one will notice if I just slip out.

I move the curtain and she calls my name weakly.

I turn to see her smile at me. "Thank you," she mouths the words.

Nodding, I turn from the small room and head back to—well—there is nowhere else I want to be. But here with Gretchen isn't where she needs me.

CHAPTER 8

Four Years Ago

GRETCHEN

I can feel the heat in my cheeks. The entire restaurant is looking at me as my friends sing *Happy Birthday*.

Levi is carrying a pink cake my way, adorned with fondant shaped like perfume bottles, lipsticks, shoes, and a tiara.

Pressing my fingers to my lips, I have to hold back tears. He's all about celebrating in big style, and he makes me feel special. He has since that first day I walked into the classroom and he was there.

My mom isn't fond of his ponytail, but I think it's sexy. Not that Levi and I see each other in that way. Well, no one sees me in that way.

I'm perfectly comfortable in my skin, but my mother finds it necessary to worry about my weight, "around all those sweets," she says.

I'm not a girl who is going to starve myself in an industry as decadent as the food industry. I'm also not going to mind myself in front of my friends. I'm having an enormous slice of that cake and one of those snowflake cupcakes on the other table too.

Levi sets the cake down in front of me and kisses the top of my head. "Make a wish, princess."

I laugh. "There are no candles."

"You don't need candles to make a wish. Just close your eyes and wish."

I close my eyes, but I already know my wish is coming true. And I can't wait to share it with him.

* * *

"You're radiant for twenty-five," Levi says nudging me with his elbow on our walk home from the restaurant that our friends opened a few months ago. "Birthdays look good on you."

"I'm radiant because I've had multiple drinks and eaten two pieces of birthday cake," I tell him, letting myself sway against him.

"Is that it?"

I nod and he shakes his head.

"I don't think so. You're always radiant," he says, and I notice that his voice has dipped into that serious mode.

I shift him a glance and smile. He always makes me feel good about myself. Perhaps that's why I keep him around as a friend. That, and his recipe for buttercream frosting.

As we walk toward my place, I stop in front of a vacant storefront and turn to look in the windows.

"What do you think?" I ask him.

Levi looks up at the building, and then joins me at the window. "I think it's empty."

I laugh. "What do you think of this as my bakery?"

I expected him to daydream with me, but he steps back. A

line forms between his brows, and he runs his fingers over his top lip.

"You're thinking about opening your own bakery?"

I'm not sure why he's so wigged out by that. It's always been my dream.

"Yes."

"You're not ready."

All the excitement that had been bubbling up inside me now has me sick.

"Who says I'm not ready?" I counter back.

"I say."

I start walking again, and Levi hurries to catch up with me. I may be short, but my legs move fast.

He reaches for me and turns me toward him.

"Gretchen, I'm sorry," he says.

"No, you're not. You mean it."

"I just—"

"You just got a lucky break, so it's okay for you to run your own place before you're thirty? But the rest of us don't amount to one Levi Braddock? So, my dreams are irrelevant?"

"Gretch," he breathes out the shortened version of my name.

Taking both of my hands, he holds them in his to our sides, and leans his forehead against mine.

"This isn't how I wanted this night to end," he says.

"You had something else horrible you wanted to say to me?"

With his forehead still against mine, he shakes his head. "No. I wanted to ask you to come to work for me."

I take a step back from him. "Seriously?"

"Yes."

Everything inside of me is all mixed up. I love what I do, and I'm really good at it. Levi and I work together all the time, so that's not the problem. But if I worked for him, I'd never leave. I can't be under him, supervised. I need to do my own thing, and my parents have made it so I can do that.

"That's quite an honor," I say.

"Would you consider it?"

I bite down on my lip and look back at the storefront we'd walked past. I take his hand in mine and move back toward the dark front door.

"No," I say, as I look through the window at the dirty, dark space. "This is what I want, Levi. My parents have offered to help me."

His hand releases from mine, and a moment later, his arms come around me from behind, and he leans his chin on my shoulder.

"You're going to be wildly popular down here among the office workers with your pastries and cupcakes. And I know there won't be a bride in all of Colorado who isn't going to flock to your door for her wedding cake."

He's sincere.

I turn to face him, but he doesn't release me, so now I'm in his arms and pressed against him. My instinct is to wrap my arms around his neck.

We've been friends since we met at the culinary school over a year ago. When I graduated, he took me out to celebrate. When I got my first job, we celebrated again.

I'm used to being this close to the man, but this feels different. Whatever is surging through me isn't just the comfort of my friend holding me. My breath is heavy. His breath is heavy.

"There's more," he says, his voice low and close to my ear.

"What?"

Levi moves his hands from my hips and cups my face. His eyes lock on mine, and he studies me. "I want to give you this," he says before he lowers his lips to mine and kisses me.

That breath that was heavy in my chest is now stuck there as my lips become pliant under his.

Levi tucks his hands up into my hair, then trails his fingers down the sides of my throat.

Need moves through me, and I push myself closer to him, as his hands move down my sides and wrap around me.

What have we done? We're friends. I've counted on this friendship for over a year. Everything in this moment has changed us.

When Levi eases back, he presses his forehead to mine again, and we both fight for breath.

"That's what you wanted to give me for my birthday?" I manage as I open my eyes.

"Yes. I couldn't keep my feelings to myself any longer. You needed to know how I was feeling."

"It's a lot to take in."

"Is it?" he asks, pressing another quick kiss to my lips. "You didn't know?"

"I never assume anyone is interested in me. Look at me," I say, but he doesn't step back.

"I've been looking for a long time, Gretch. You're the loveliest woman I've ever known."

I swallow hard. I can feel tears beginning to burn the backs of my eyes. "You really think that?"

"I do."

My knees are weaker than they were when he kissed me.

"What does this mean?"

The corner of his mouth curls up and that dimple, oh that dimple, pops. "I want us to be together. That's what it means. Even if you don't come to work for me, I want to be us."

"Us," I repeat.

"When people talk about us, I want it to be Gretchen and Levi. Levi and Gretchen."

"You're asking me to be your girlfriend?"

He trails his fingers down my throat again, but now he's grinning. "You've always been my girlfriend," he says. "I just want to make it official. I just want to know you want this too."

I don't really have to think about it. I've always been attracted to him. I just never thought someone as charismatic as Levi Braddock would want to be with me—not like that.

"I do want that," I admit.

Levi lets out a breath. "Thank goodness. You had me worried that I was laying my heart on the line." He reaches into his pocket and pulls out one of the plastic snowflake rings that had adorned the cupcakes on the other table at dinner. "I got this for you. Remember what you told me about talent and snowflakes?"

"They're all similar, but each is as unique as a snowflake."

"Just like you're unique." He slips the ring on my pinkie and then kisses my hand. "I'd considered carrying some mistletoe with me too in case the kiss went badly, and I had to fake it," he teases.

"I guess this wasn't our first kiss, was it?"

"It's the official first kiss of *us*."

I step back so that I can look him in the eye. "I'm all in, on this us thing," I say. "But I still won't work for you."

He nods. "I know. And I'll be right here helping you become my competition," he laughs. "You're going to be extremely successful."

"You think so?"

"I do. I don't know anyone else in the world with more talent than you. It's only one of the reasons I love you."

I take another step back at the sound of those words. "You love me?"

Levi gathers me back into his arms. "Oh, Gretchen," he says, using my full name. "There has never been a day when I didn't love you."

CHAPTER 9

Present

LEVI

Checking my watch—five A.M.—and looking around the bakery, I realize that the morning came along, and I wasn't really part of it.

My staff is busy making muffins and pastries to sell to those headed off to work later this morning. Aerial has been busy getting the cupcake order finalized for the casino. And I have been standing in the middle of it not doing a damn thing.

I pinch the bridge of my nose.

"Everything okay this morning?" Aerial asks as she moves a tower of cupcakes toward the loading door.

I nod. "Long night."

She chuckles. "You haven't had a long night in a long time. I see that we got some bags of flour. Any coincidence that we have flour and you didn't get any sleep?"

"Actually, yes."

Her eyes grow wide, and her smile matches, but fades when I shake my head.

"Nothing as romantic as you're thinking," I tell her. "Gretchen was in a car accident and—"

Aerial's hand is on my arm. "Is she okay?"

"She dislocated her shoulder and has some cuts and bruises."

"You were with her?" There's a hopeful tone in her voice again.

"It happened right out front. She brought the flour, then got rear ended, fairly hard, I might add."

"That's terrible. You stayed with her."

"I ran out and got her help. I went to the hospital until Marsha could get there."

Aerial shakes her head. "Was she glad to see you?"

I wrinkle my nose. "Is she ever?"

Aerial gives me a playful shrug. "She holds a grudge. You piss her off once and she holds on to it forever."

She pushes the trays toward the door and makes marks on her clipboard.

Aerial would know what she's talking about. Gretchen hasn't talked to her for years either. Though, if I recall, that argument was over a man, and long before I managed to get on the wrong side of Gretchen Meyers.

The drive up through the canyon to the casino is exactly what I need to calm myself after not being able to sleep last night. I'd hoped Marsha would call me and let me know how Gretchen was, but she hadn't. Of course, Gretchen hadn't called me herself either.

The member of my staff that I had drive up to the casino with me has had his headphones in the entire drive. He hasn't said a word. I can't decide if it's because my head is in the clouds, or if my head is in the clouds because he's not talking to me.

As I pull into the loading area at the casino, I see Gretchen's delivery van. I know how badly she was hurt, and it won't surprise me if I see her—but it will piss me off.

"Hey, Levi," one of the young men on Gretchen's staff calls out to me with a nod. I return the gesture.

I see enough of those go-getters come through the culinary school when I teach, but I don't remember many of their names. They land in local bakeries, and I see them from time to time. Occasionally one of them will take their education and make a career of it. But, like most schools, the percentage of those who try it out and move on is higher.

Gretchen was one of those who shone from the moment she walked through the doors. She knew what she was going to do, and thus far, she's stayed on track. She's brilliant, and I always thought I'd get to be part of her life while she became one of the most sought-after pastry chefs in Denver, but that wasn't in the stars for us.

As the young man comes out for another tray, I move toward the van. "Have you heard from Gretchen this morning?"

He shakes his head. "Marsha said she was in some accident. She called us all in to pick up the slack."

I had to chuckle at that. It would take her entire staff to pick up pieces, I thought. Gretchen is hands-on. That's how she likes it.

"She'll be back soon enough. Can I help you carry in some trays?"

"This is the last one. I have them all in and Bethany is setting up the display. *Charlotte's Goodies* was here first, and their display is fancy. I think I'm glad Gretchen didn't see it."

That makes me wince. "Yeah, all the better. Have a safe drive down the canyon," I tell him with a wave as I walk inside to see where I'm supposed to set up.

Bella, the tall, thin woman who always has a pen in her

hand in lieu of a cigarette, hurries toward me. "I'm so glad you're here. It's pretty exciting to be opening under a new name," she says, sweeping her arms out to encompass the casino that changes its name every year and reopens with all the glory of a new business.

"Very exciting indeed," I say, to appease her.

"Charlotte was here early, and that woman makes me crazy."

"Maybe it's time to stop using her huh?" I wink and Bella laughs.

"The management likes the competition you all bring to the table. But she's pushy, and I'd be happy if all her cupcakes fell on the floor," she whispers. "Did you hear Gretchen was in some kind of accident? I mean, she sent her staff and didn't come at all. Do you suppose that really happened? It doesn't show well for her."

This is the side of business that I don't like, the speculation on someone who has done nothing but be an outstanding businessperson. But I have to consider that Charlotte was the first to talk to Bella this morning. Who knows what she had to say.

"She was in fact in an accident. I was there. She's okay, but she dislocated her shoulder and has some stitches."

Bella's expression changes. Her blue eyes soften, and she presses her hand to her chest. "That's horrible. I hope she's okay."

"She will be. Marsha is taking good care of her. You'll be hearing from her soon, don't you worry."

"It sounds like she's in good hands then. I'll make sure management sends a card."

That's the least they could do, I think as I smile at Bella.

"Why don't you show me where you need me to set up, and I'll get out of your hair too."

Resting her hand on my arm, she smiles up at me. "We'd

use you for everything, you know. I don't know why they make me use all three of you."

I try to compose my reply to be gracious. "We all appreciate your business. You keep changing the name of the casino and I'll keep showing up."

She laughs and leads me to the room where they have the tables ready for food, and the cupcakes are displayed.

Charlotte's display is ornate and gaudy. I will guarantee more than one person puts their sleeve into a cupcake. They are tastefully decorated, and if they were displayed alone, no one would notice that they dull in comparison to Gretchen's.

Sometimes I think it's best to show up last. I can set up knowing what my competition brought to the table—literally.

"I know she didn't come personally, but she certainly has an eye for design," Bella says as we stand in front of Gretchen's table.

"I taught her everything I know," I tease and Bella laughs.

"Something tells me she knew what she was doing before she met you."

That was true enough. Even when Gretchen was my student, there were times I learned from her.

As I look over the cupcake designs on her table, I know that she'll always strive to be better than me, and most of the time she is. I can only imagine where we'd be if we'd actually been partners—and were still lovers.

CHAPTER 10

Present

GRETCHEN

My shoulder is in constant pain, and every other muscle in my body aches too. I look around the ornate home of Olive Darling—well, her parents' home—and I figure I'm a sight.

I tried to do my hair so that it covers the stitches on my forehead, but there's no escaping the bruising around my eyes, or the fact that my arm is in a sling.

Marsha sets her hand on my bouncing leg. "You need to relax. This will go easier if you relax," she says again.

"I can't help it," I say as Olive Darling and her mother sweep into the room on an air of elegance and grace.

The petite blonde in a floral dress is grinning until she sees me when I stand.

"Oh, Gretchen. What happened?" Her hands go to her mouth.

"I was in a car accident last night," I say.

Olive and her mother exchange glances, and then both

look back at me. "We certainly could have rescheduled," Olive says.

"No. I'm fine. This is Marsha, my assistant," I say, and Marsha shakes both women's hands.

We all sit at the dining room table and Marsha turns my design book around so that Olive and her mother can look at it.

"See, Mom, I told you she was the most amazing designer ever."

Her mother nods. "These are quite lovely. You can accommodate five hundred with a cake?"

I've learned to smile at whatever number is thrown my way. "We have many options, from larger cakes, multiple cakes, or an elegant cake and trays of cupcakes."

Her mother waves off the cupcake comment. "Cakes only. Cupcakes are for sharing in preschool," she says as she turns the page in my book.

It's not the first time I've heard comments like these, and I've learned to steel myself against them.

"These are so beautiful," Olive says delighted as she turns each page. "These are so much prettier than *others'* cakes."

Once they get to the end of the book, I shift another folder toward them. "This is a concept design I drew up for you from our first discussion."

The moment Olive looks at it, her eyes go wide. Her mother, on the other hand narrows her eyes at the design.

"Oh, this is so beautiful," Olive nearly squeals.

"You need to look at more designs," her mother said matter-of-factly.

"This is exactly what I told her I wanted," Olive counters. "This is the cake."

Luckily, her mother's phone chimes and she excuses herself from the meeting.

Olive places her hands over the cake rendering. "This is

what I want. It has to feed five hundred, but this is what I want."

I nod as Marsha begins to take notes.

"I'll enhance the tiers and side cakes to accommodate, and will send you more designs," I say.

Olive taps her fingertips together in a silent clap. "May I show you a picture?"

"Of course."

Olive pulls out her phone and scrolls through the pictures. When she turns the phone around, and shows me the picture, I do everything in my power not to react.

"This is beautiful," I say, swallowing down any comments I might have.

Olive leans in. "I used to date a pastry chef in Chicago, years ago. This was one of his designs. Things didn't work out, obviously," she says pulling back her phone and gazing down at the photo. "But this was the kind of cake I've always wanted. I do like your take on the design, though. It's perfect."

Marsha knocks her knee into mine, but I don't pay her any attention. I know who the pastry chef in Chicago was, and I know the design of the cake like I know my own designs.

"We'd love to work with you and be part of your magical day. But, like your mother said. You should seek out many designs and—"

Olive leans in again. "I don't care what my mother says. This is what I want. I'm signing the contracts. I'm in charge."

"Then it sounds like we should finalize plans," I say, and then Marsha takes over.

* * *

As Marsha pulls away from the enormous house in Cherry Hills, she pounds her hand to the steering wheel.

"Did Olive Darling actually show you a cake design from Levi Braddock?"

I nod, adjusting my arm in the sling.

"You're not fazed by this. Why are you not fazed by this?" She's nearly screaming and laughing at the same time.

"Because I knew they dated in Chicago."

Shaking her head as she comes to the end of the driveway, she looks at me and smiles. "You didn't take the opportunity to let Olive know you're an ex too and commiserate in hating the man?"

"The less she knows about me, the better off I am. Besides, do you know the publicity this is going to bring us? The quarterback and the coach's daughter? It doesn't matter if the marriage lasts. We just need a few pictures of the cake to make it into People magazine or onto ESPN or E! My past shouldn't interfere with this sale, just as Olive's past shouldn't interfere with it either."

"I didn't mean to tell him about your meeting with her. I didn't cause a problem when I did that, did I?"

I shake my head and slide on my sunglasses. "No. In fact, he said when Olive saw what I could do, I'd be her only choice. I'm not sure she even knows he's in Denver."

"How could she not know? He's food industry royalty."

I shrug my good shoulder. "He's also national food industry royalty. He could be anywhere. I'm not going to worry about it. His misfortune is going to be my golden ticket. Be prepared to start working with some of the elite."

"We do work with the elite," Marsha says.

"Not the kind I'm thinking. But we're about to," I say.

Yes, Olive Darling's wedding cake is going to be legendary, and the whole world is going to see it.

CHAPTER 11

3 years ago

GRETCHEN

My name is painted on the window in elegant letters. *Gretchen Meyers Bakery*. I'd wept the first time I saw it, and again the second time.

But standing in front of the store which will open in a week, looking at the name now with Levi's arms wrapped around me, it hits different.

I've never been so happy in my entire life.

"You've done it," he whispers in my ear. "You're about to make history, sweetheart."

"I feel absolutely sick."

"It's normal. I promise," he says as he brushes my lips with his. "Take me for a tour."

I laugh, running my fingers through his short hair, which looks equally as sexy on him as his long hair had.

"You want a tour? You've been in here a million times already."

"I've never been in it a week from your grand opening

with your name on the window. Show me what you've created."

I slip my arms around him and look up into those dark and mesmerizing eyes. "Before we go in, I just want to say thank you. I couldn't have done this without you."

"I didn't have anything to do with—"

I silence him with a kiss. "But you have. Since the minute I sat down at that table at the culinary school, you've been right by my side."

"Because I knew you were going to be the one to put all of your competition to shame. Including me."

"I've learned so much from you." I lift my hands to his face. "I love you, Levi. This place makes me so happy, but having you here to share it with me, I can't even describe the joy I feel."

"I will always be here for you. No matter what," he promises.

I playfully lift my brow. "No matter what?"

"Even if you become wildly popular, and start taking over my appearances on TV, or those big-ticket clients, I'll still be right here if you need me."

I laugh. "I don't think I'll ever be on TV," I say, because I'm not sure anyone wants to see someone who looks like me on TV. Levi on the other hand, he's dynamic and gorgeous. "And as for those big-ticket clients, there's enough of them to go around."

"Optimistic. It's only one of your wonderful traits. By the way, I got you something for your door," he reaches into his pocket and pulls out a plastic sprig of mistletoe.

I laugh as I take it from him. "Why?"

"The way I look at it, I kissed you as you walked out of one bakery, and I'm kissing you as you're walking into another. It carries good memories."

I look at the mistletoe he's placed in my hand. "Mistletoe memories, huh?"

"It's cheeky, but you are my competition. I can't be too serious about all this."

I laugh as I hold the mistletoe over my head and he kisses me gently, then says, "I love you."

* * *

As I look around the front end of my bakery, now filled with those who came to celebrate me, I press a hand to my jittery stomach.

I've been immersed in the Denver culinary scene for two years now, made a name for myself, and those who came to see what I built have all been there for it. I've been to many of their restaurant openings or worked catering jobs when they needed me. And now here they all are celebrating me.

Charlotte declined my invitation, of course. When I told her of my plans, she fired me on the spot. Levi didn't take the opportunity to say *I told you so*, but I'm sure he was thinking it. Had she only hired me to keep me from competing with her? Was she afraid of my skill? That's what Levi had said. *Keep your friends close, and your enemies closer.*

The more I get to thinking about it, she never shows up to soft or grand openings. I have to assume that no one invites her.

Levi's arms wrap around me from behind, and I jump. I'm in my own world watching our friends enjoy themselves in my bakery.

His chin rests on my shoulder. "You're going to do well here," he says softly in my ear. "Marsha told me she's taken eight orders from restaurants for breads, rolls, and pastries."

I let out a steadying breath. "That's a lot."

"It's just a start." He lifted a finger to point to our friends

Jill and Sarah by the door. "You need to make your way over there and look at the rock on Sarah's finger. Jill proposed a week ago, and they need a wedding cake."

I turn in his arms and stare at him. "Oh, God!"

"You're ready for this. You've made masterpieces that I never could have, no matter how many years of experience I have. It's time for you to shine, baby."

I place my hands on his cheeks and pull him toward me, laying a hard kiss on his lips. "Thank you."

"For what?"

"We're competition now, and yet, you're right here supporting me—loving me."

"I don't ever plan to do any different." He lifts his head as someone else walks through the door, and he waves.

I turn to see Aerial walk through the front door and begin to greet people.

"What is she doing here?" I ask through gritted teeth.

"I invited her. She's not going to bite, and you can be cordial."

Levi takes my hand, and we walk through the people who reach out to me to congratulate me. He walks toward Jill and Sarah, and Aerial has stopped to talk to them.

"Ladies," he says, leaning to kiss all three of them on the cheeks.

Jill reaches out a hand to touch my arm. "This is magnificent, Gretchen. Just magnificent. Congratulations."

"Thank you," I say, squeezing Levi's hand. "I hear congratulations are in order for you as well."

Sarah holds up her hand and wiggles her ring finger. "She proposed and I said yes," she squeals, and wraps an arm around Jill. "We also want to talk cake."

"I'd be happy to discuss a cake design with you," I say, but I notice Aerial's expression becomes one of confusion as she shifts her eyes to Levi, who shakes his head slightly.

What did I miss?

"I'll talk to Marsha," Sarah says. "I know she has your schedule."

"She does."

My name is called from across the store and I move from the small group discussing wedding cakes. But as I'm drawn into another conversation, Aerial has Levi's attention and the more she talks, the more he nods.

When we were roommates back in culinary school, Aerial dated the only guy I was ever interested in, before Levi. Sure, it wasn't as if she stole the guy out from under me, but he was interested. Then she came around, and suddenly they were a thing. A few years later, they got married. I refused the invite to the wedding.

Yes, I'm that petty.

She's worked for Levi for a while now, and they're a good team. But looking at her now, leaned into him, I wonder if she's starting to make a move on him. I mean, I can't blame her, but I don't know what to think. I know she's happily married, and maybe this is just a show for me, because she's petty too.

Levi looks back in my direction and gives me a smile and a wink. He still loves me. I know he does. Whatever she's plotting it's just not going to work.

CHAPTER 12

Present

GRETCHEN

Popping a mini candy bar into my mouth, from the plastic pumpkin on my workstation, I stand back and look at the reindeer prototype. He's perfect, and freaking expensive.

I've been working on him for months, and he's turning out just as I'd imagined.

My brother helped me create the skeletal parts to the cake. He's a genius, though if I tell him that to his face, he gets a big head. The nose lights up, the fondant for the hide is the right shade, and I finally got the color of the hooves just the way I want it. I have one month to perfect anything that isn't just right, and to amass my ingredients to recreate him.

"I think he's perfect," Marsha says, standing next to me with a clipboard full of notes I've just rattled off to her.

"He is. He really is." I might sound pretentious, but I just don't care.

After my car accident, I wasn't sure I could pull this off, but I did it. Not only did I create a masterpiece for the

Hermon's of Denver Hotel, but I was also interviewed by a wedding magazine about Olive Darling's upcoming cake. It's all happening—that success that I've always dreamed of.

"Okay, now put your toys away. You need to get home and get ready," Marsha presses the clipboard to her chest.

"Right. Soft opening."

She nods. "Are you sure you don't want to call in a date?"

Still looking at my creation, I shake my head. "I've been to hundreds of these events. I don't need a date."

"I'll get this covered up and in the cooler. You get going."

I'm still smiling at the enormous cake as I walk back to my office and gather my things.

An hour later, I pull up to the front of *Sebastian's Bistro*. He's pulled out all the stops. There's even a valet waiting for me to leave my car. I step out, hand the keys to the valet, and wrap my shawl around my shoulders to ward off the October chill.

The outside of the old building has lights adorning the awning and crawling up to the second floor. There is music pouring from inside, and already the people are shoulder to shoulder. Soft opening, my foot. This is an all-out grand opening party.

"Gretchen, darling," Sebastian moves right to me and kisses me on both cheeks. He's in his black chef's coat with his name embroidered on the front.

"This is beautiful," I compliment as he continues to hold me.

"It is. It's going to put Devon to shame."

I can't help but draw in my lips when he talks about his ex-partner in that way, but Devon deserves it. He broke Sebastian's heart into a million pieces, forcing him to start over. But, looking around, Sebastian made the best of it.

He eases back, now taking hold of my hands. "You look beautiful. I heard you'd been in an accident."

"I got rear ended."

Sebastian shakes his head. "Stupid drivers."

I can't help but grin up at him.

"Did you bring a date?" he asks, looking behind me.

"No."

"You should have. You should have brought some hunky man to show off."

That causes me to laugh. "I don't have a hunky man to show off. I work too hard."

He puckers his lips. "Didn't stop you-know-who."

I shrug at his comment, and he leans in to talk into my ear.

"Levi Braddock is here and he's with someone," he whispers loudly into my ear. "She's overdone. She's clinging to him as if he might take a breath without her. She's not you, darling. It should be you."

I swallow hard and shake my head. "That was over a long time ago."

He makes a dismissive noise as if he doesn't buy that at all, but it's true. No matter how weak my knees go when I see the man, I'm not interested in going through that again.

Someone draws Sebastian's attention away from me, and I move further into the restaurant and head toward the bar. I always allow myself one drink at these openings, and no more.

I order a wine spritzer and turn to see Levi standing next to me, that million-dollar smile aimed right at me. It's only been three months since I've seen him, but his hair is longer again. I hate that he's so sexy.

"You look better than when I saw you last," he says lifting his wine glass to his lips.

"I'm sure I do." Taking the drink that the bartender hands me, I consider what I need to say to the man in front of me. "I never thanked you for everything you did for me that night. I appreciated it."

I took him by surprise, by the way his eyes go wide for a moment and that grin turns up the corner of his mouth.

"You know I'd do anything for you," he says, and instead of being sincere, I want to lash out at him for saying such a thing.

But I don't get my chance. A blonde woman in a slinky dress moves in next to him and moves as if to mold her body to his. Crazily enough, he looks at me as if he's a bit uncomfortable with the attention, but she doesn't notice. Her eyes are lasers set on me.

"I missed you," she coos into his ear. "Did you get me a drink?"

I'm going to be sick.

Levi nods and hands her a glass of wine.

"Who is this?" she pouts.

"This is an old friend," is all he says. He obviously knows the woman hanging on him well enough to know she couldn't care less about my name. "Why don't you go get a plate of hors d'oeuvres, and I'll keep our place at the bar."

The woman scans one more look over me as if she's afraid I'll take off with Levi. Fat chance.

We both watch her walk away, and I shake my head. It's a reaction that shouldn't even have surfaced, but I can't help myself.

"Would you like to see the kitchen?" Levi asks.

"Your date will be right back."

His nostrils flare. "I think she put a magnet in my pocket. I have no doubt she'll find me."

I can't help but laugh at that as I sip my wine.

When I first met Levi, he was no stranger to attracting women. He had long hair, those dark sexy eyes, and a charisma to him that just had women falling all over him.

It was part of the reason he was easy to watch on TV, and his appearances on cooking shows and news segments boosted his popularity.

Heck, it didn't take long for me to fall for him too—but I'd thought I was different.

"I'm sure Sebastian will show me around," I say.

Levi moves closer to me, takes my free hand, linking our fingers, and leads me away from the bar. I guess I should have just said no.

We weave through people, some of whom I don't want to see us holding hands. No one around remembers when this was an amicable relationship. Everyone in this restaurant knows that he lied to me. Stole my idea. Banked on it.

I pull my hand from his, and he looks down at me as if I'd kicked him.

"Seriously. What are you doing?" I ask over the crowd.

"I'm taking you to see the kitchen."

"We have to hold hands to do that?"

Levi purses his lips. "I didn't mean to—"

"I'm sure you didn't," I say with as much sarcasm as I can possibly muster. "Everyone is staring at us."

"We're friends."

I blink hard. "When did we establish that?"

His lips form a tight line, and he grabs my hand again. This time, he drags me into the kitchen, and down a tight hallway.

"We are friends, Gretch. We've always been friends," he says as if he completely believes it.

I almost spill my wine when I take in a breath that shakes my entire body. "Are you kidding me?"

"Would you have brought an enemy flour when they needed it? No. You brought it to a friend. And would an enemy help you from a wrecked car? No."

"You're delusional."

Levi runs his hand over his hair. "I'm not. I don't want you to hate me for the rest of my life."

"Then you shouldn't have—"

He lifts his fingers to my lips to stop me. "I know," he says stepping in closer, close enough our bodies are touching.

The fingers he had silenced my words with brush across my lips. "I know," he says again.

His eyes lock on mine and he inches in even closer until his lips are only a breath away.

I can feel the heat of his breath, smell the wine.

He's not going to kiss me, I say to myself, but not one muscle in my body moves to stop him.

"Gretchen? Levi?" The voice squeals from the kitchen, but it's not his date. It's a voice I'm familiar with.

We both turn our heads, cheeks brushing because we're so close, to see Olive Darling standing just beyond us with her hand over her mouth.

"Olive," I say as I move from Levi. "I didn't know you'd—"

"I can't believe what I'm seeing. You and Levi?" Her eyes dart to him. "What are you doing here?"

I can feel him standing right behind me now, and I'm not so sure his hand isn't on the small of my back. But considering that every nerve ending in my body is triggered, I just don't know.

"I live in Denver. I have for years," he says with some humor.

"And you and Gretchen?" Olive puts her fingers to her lips. "I can't have you design my wedding cake now," she says looking right at me.

I can feel the blood drain from my head. "Olive, this isn't anything. We're not—"

"I cancel my order," she says on a sob. "I'll find a new bakery."

CHAPTER 13

Present

LEVI

Olive hurries from Sebastian's kitchen with her hands waving in hysterics, and sobs so loud that the entire kitchen staff has turned to look at her.

Gretchen turns and shoves me. I stumble back into the wall. I'm waiting for her to come at me with a string of curses, but there is nothing but sheer anger in her eyes.

She turns and calls after Olive, and I stand in the kitchen worried that this strange, little dilemma is going to cost Sebastian in the end.

But a man doesn't hide in the kitchen when there are two very distraught women, who both hate him, about to have a cat fight.

If I ever cared for either of them, I needed to follow them.

The noise in the dining room had dimmed considerably. Olive was standing next to a giant of a man, and Gretchen was hurrying toward her.

I manage my way through the crowd, smiling as if I'm

perfectly calm, but I'm not. There is something raging inside of me, and I have to imagine it matches the rage of the women about to have words.

"Olive, please give me a moment to explain," I hear Gretchen say as I walk toward the women and the enormous man.

"I don't want to hear it. I would never have chosen your bakery if—"

The enormous man points a finger in my direction. "Oh, man, I've seen you on TV," he says with an overabundance of enthusiasm. Obviously, he's unaware of the mess he's standing in.

I swallow hard and nod. "Yes. Likewise, I've seen you on TV too."

He laughs as if he's at some frat party. Then I remember that Olive Darling is marrying the quarterback of the football team. I couldn't care less about football, and I can't even think of his name.

The man holds out an enormous hand to shake mine. I lift my hand to accept, and the man's hand swallows mine. Olive's taste in men has changed considerably since I left her in Chicago.

"Brock Adams," he says as he pumps my arm up and down.

"Levi Braddock," I say, and his eyes go wide. Now I'm worried for my wellbeing.

"No, way. You beat Bobby Flay!" he cheers, and both women look up at him with wide eyes.

"Brock," Olive bites out his name through gritted teeth. "This is Levi—you know, Le-vi," she breaks my name down for him as if it'll make him understand the situation.

He thinks on it for a moment, his hand still gripping mine. "Oh," Brock says low. "And this is your cake girl?"

Olive nods impatiently.

"Dang. Maybe we should step outside and talk," the man says as he finally drops my hand. At least he has common sense.

I take that as my cue to escort *my lady* out the front door, as he wraps an arm around Olive and starts for the door as well.

"Levi?"

I let out a breath and turn to see my date scurrying toward the four of us as we make our way to the door. Sebastian steps in, grinning.

"You're not all leaving, are you?" he asks as he scans a look over his celebrity couple, and then his eyes fall to Gretchen and me, and grow wide. "You're leaving together?"

My date squeals behind me. "You're leaving with her?"

"We're just stepping outside to have a conversation," I assure Sebastian, and my date.

Sebastian's face softens and he smiles. "I'm glad to see you talking."

Oh, if he only knew, I thought as we walked past him, my date in tow.

Because the party poured out of the restaurant and onto the sidewalk, we walk down the street. When we stop, Olive turns around and points at me.

"You're ruining my life!" she shouts in my direction.

Her building of a fiancé pulls her closer to him. "Now, sweetie—"

"I mean it."

Feeling as if I need to defend myself from this accusation, I hold up my hand as if I must request permission to speak. "I didn't ruin your life."

Gretchen folds her arms in front of herself. "Yes, Levi, please explain how you think you didn't ruin her life."

Now, that's not helpful.

I'm not sure Gretchen and I ever had the conversation

about Olive and me, other than I'd dated her. Because if we had, she wouldn't have just hung that noose around my neck with her words.

I run my tongue over my teeth and collect myself. Standing in front of me are the two women I've ever given any part of my heart to, and they both hate me. The date I brought to the opening, whom I've known all of a week, and brought just because I thought it was time to venture back into the dating pool, is standing just beyond the circle with wide eyes. The giant of a fiancé wrapped around Olive could kill me now, and there wouldn't be a soul in that entire restaurant brave enough to stop him. But he seems to be on my side, for the moment. I assume that if he's marrying the debutante princess, he already knows she's a bit on the dramatic side.

Focusing on Gretchen, I form my story. "I don't think I ruined her life, because I left her life. I walked out. I moved across the country. I took everything with me—meaning my belongings and my status at the time."

Olive lets out some kind of grunt, and everyone turns their eyes to her.

"That's your story?" she scoffs. "You broke my heart."

"You were caught with another guy, and it was splashed all over the local news at a time when I was building my reputation in Chicago."

I notice the fiancé easing his protective grip on her. Maybe I shouldn't have spurted that out, but how could I help it at that point? Besides, if he just did one google search on his precious fiancée, it'd all show up.

Olive's eyes grow wide. Yep, I just outed her.

I may be brilliant with pastries, but this has often been my problem around women.

Though, I do notice that Gretchen's lips are tight. Is she trying to hold in a laugh? Had this softened the blow of the loss of the job?

Olive opens her mouth to speak, closes it, and then takes in a breath. Tears are welling in her eyes. "You just took off."

"I sure did," I confess.

"And you took the cat."

If I don't control myself, I'll lose my composure too, and laugh. I'll bet if I ask, she can't even name that cat.

"That's her cat?" Gretchen asks, her voice strained against the laugh she's holding in.

"It was our cat, and I took care of him," I confirm.

"My cat. My cat!" Olive shouts, and Brock shushes her.

"Our cat," I confirm.

I haven't said a word to Olive in nearly ten years, not until we started this conversation on the street. I hadn't wanted my life to be about the press and who I was dating back then. I was rising in my field, and yes, I'd beaten Bobby Flay at twenty-three years old. She was all about the high life and what it gave to her. I just wanted to be the best at what I did.

It was always inevitable that it would end, but I'll admit, I hadn't thought it would end as it had.

"Yes, I took the cat," I say, and hadn't she run to the press with that story too? But no one cared as much about the cat I took off with as they had about her new love affair. I think I got lucky when I hightailed it out of Chicago.

"Why don't we go get you a drink?" the fiancé says as he turns Olive back to the restaurant. "We don't want everyone looking this way."

Yeah, Brock Adams is smarter than he looks. He can call the plays, no matter what they might be.

Gretchen's tight lips turn into a pucker. "I'm thinking that I would have lost that job no matter what."

"I'm not sure they'll make it to the altar, unless they're both just craving the press."

Gretchen shrugs. "There is that. They do love their publicity." Finally, she turns to me. "I'm sorry I was so nasty. I just assumed that—"

"Most of the problem between you and I was always assumption."

With that, and the thought that I almost kissed Gretchen Meyers in the hallway, and that alone should be the high I walk out on, I tuck my hands into my pockets and walk back into the restaurant to say goodbye to Sebastian. I think I've had enough drama for one night.

When someone pulls at my arm, I remember I have a date. It might be a good time to take her home and call it a night.

CHAPTER 14

2 Years Ago

LEVI

Gretchen is a workaholic, and I thought I was bad. My bakery has been closed for hours, and I've been sitting in hers watching her create a cake that deep inside I'm lustful over.

Keeping my pride in check with my jealousy looming is an ongoing battle, because I've always said Gretchen is more talented than anyone I've ever known, including myself.

Last week I taped a baking battle episode for a national cooking channel, and I won. But the interview questions had all been about my beautiful girlfriend/business competitor. She's making a name for herself rather quickly.

"What do you think?" Gretchen steps back from her workstation, wrapping her fingers in the towel at her waist. She chews on that plump bottom lip, and all I want to do is chew on it as well.

I move from where I've been perched on a stool, watching her for over an hour, and walk to her.

Lifting my hand to her cheek, I take my moment with

those lips, kissing her softly and enjoying the feel of her against me. When I ease back, her eyes blink hard before she shakes her head with a smile.

"You're distracting me," she says, then nods at the cake. "What do you think?"

"I think it's a masterpiece. I think you're going to get the contract and be even busier than you already are. I think the world is ready to know your name. I think you should have my name," I say, but honestly, I don't even know where that came from, except straight from my heart.

"First of all," she says, and then swallows hard. "You haven't even turned around and looked at the cake."

"I've been looking at it for an hour."

She nods, and her expression changes to serious. "What do you mean, I should have your name?"

I back her up until she has to sit on the stool behind her. Moving in between her thighs, she wraps her legs around me and I pull her in.

Lowering my mouth to hers, I take what she offers. She's still as sweet as the first time I kissed her in Charlotte's doorway under the mistletoe, and again in her own doorway on her birthday.

We've hung mistletoe in our apartment above the door and above the bed so that we never leave or go to bed without kissing. It may seem childish, or perhaps wrought in tradition.

Gretchen Meyers is my biggest competition and my only desire, and it's a crazy mix. On one hand she could bury my business if she wanted to. Now at twenty-nine, she's one of the most sought-after cake designers in all of Denver. I've lost business to her, but then I've enjoyed celebrating those wins for her. Of course, when she wins, Charlotte loses too, and that's become a bit of a bitter war between the two of them, and I'm in the middle of that war, but always on Gretchen's side.

When I ease back, those plump lips are deep in color, and begging me to kiss her more.

"What do you think?" I say softly.

"You've scrambled my brain." She lets out a small laugh. "Are you really asking me to take your name?"

"Yes."

"As in, marry you?"

I nod again. "Yes. Gretchen, will you marry me?"

She swallows hard again, and her brows have drawn in. Maybe I shouldn't speak from my heart. Maybe my heart doesn't know anything. This isn't the reaction I would ever have thought I'd get, even though it wasn't thought out.

I take a breath to right the wrong, but her expression softens.

"You want me to be your wife?" she asks, as if she's clarifying all of the possibilities.

"Yes." I press another soft kiss to her lips. "Gretchen, will you be my wife?"

She licks the lips I just kissed, then bites down on the bottom one as her eyes fill with tears.

She nods and lifts her hands to cup my face. "Yes. Yes, I'll marry you and be your wife."

"I love you," I say taking possession of her mouth again. I've never been so happy in all my life, and I didn't even know this was what I wanted. But I've always known Gretchen was what I wanted. This is just logical.

As our lips part, she begins to laugh. Tears are streaming down her cheeks as she presses her fingers to her lips.

"What's so funny?" I ask.

"Who will make our wedding cake?"

I join her in the moment with laughter, wiping away her tears. My heart is so full.

The cake she's been slaving over is forgotten, all but

storing it. She's worked countless hours on it, and it is hands-down the most beautiful cake I've ever seen.

We've all been vying for the contract to be the exclusive wedding cake designer for a high-end hotel in Aspen, and by the looks of her cake, Gretchen will no doubt win that contract, and she deserves to.

I already know the executive chef doesn't like Charlotte, and the others that are looking to impress have nothing on Gretchen. It comes down to the two of us, and I know, no matter which one of us gets that contract, the other will celebrate that win.

But now, now that we're engaged, and hurrying out of the bakery to head home and celebrate what we've just agreed upon, I know no matter which of us gets that contract, it's as if we both do. Our names may be on two different bakeries, and we may compete for business, but now we're truly partners.

CHAPTER 15

Two Years Ago

GRETCHEN

I don't usually count down the hours until the bakery closes, but today I am. Christmas Eve and we've been slammed since six this morning.

Collectively, my staff and I agreed to have a big company outing to celebrate our amazing year after the new year. Instead of closing shop early, like most of the other businesses, we've pushed through, selling until the eleventh hour.

Cakes, pastries, breads, and pies have been walking out the door all day. All orders had to be placed in advance, so that we didn't have inventory laying around over the long holiday weekend, and the shelves are growing bare. We're almost out of here.

This is the first Christmas Levi and I will spend in our own place. The tree we chose is obnoxious, and so perfect. His mother brought over four boxes of antique ornaments for us to decorate with, as they were going to Europe for Christmas and wouldn't be putting up a tree.

And of course, Levi had put mistletoe at the top of the tree in lieu of the star. It seemed appropriate for another first kiss in our own place, under our own tree.

Because I'm obsessed with the tree, and watching it twinkle in the dark, I happened to have noticed the small gift tucked up between its branches. Small enough to be a ring, I think.

The very thought of it warms my insides and brings a stupid grin to my lips.

"Gretchen, Louisa Fitzpatrick asked to see you," Marsha says as she pokes her head in the doorway of my office.

Louisa is a local news reporter. She's interviewed me a couple of times as we set up cakes for influential customers, a few rock stars who were playing at Red Rocks, and a corporate cake in the shape of an airplane.

"What does she want?"

Marsha shrugged. "She has a cameraman with her."

"I'm not ready to do an interview."

Marsha smiles. "You look gloriously well worked. Your shelves are nearly bare. You're the only bakery in town still open on Christmas Eve, and you sent an enormous shipment to the shelter. Trust me, you're camera worthy," she says with some pride.

"Tell her I'll be right out," I say, and Marsha hurries away.

I collect myself, then stand from behind my desk and check myself in the mirror by the door. I'm a perfect mess, but Marsha is right. I've been working since four o'clock this morning. I look like I've put in a glorious full day.

I button up my chef coat, pinch my cheeks for some color, and wipe off the ganache I have on my cheek that no one seemed to mention.

When I walk out to the front of the bakery, Louisa is setting up for an interview shot. I take a deep breath and approach her as my staff continues to work, but grins at me, perhaps hoping to get in the shot.

The cameraman is taking video of them all working and the customers still coming in to pick up orders. Yes, this all looks good. I've done it. I've made elaborate wedding cakes for celebrities, I've designed custom cakes for corporate events and celebrations, and I have a loyal following for cinnamon rolls too. I'm not sure what's next, maybe expansion. It doesn't matter. I have everything I've ever wanted in my entire life at my fingertips, including the love of a man who cherishes me.

Louisa smiles wide as I walk toward her.

"Gretchen, you look wonderful," she says and I accept the compliment. In my head I'm thinking my hair is a mess, I don't have any makeup on, and the last time she interviewed me I was ten pounds lighter.

"Thank you."

"You're one of the only businesses left open before Christmas, can we interview you?"

Smiling graciously, I say, "Of course."

The cameraman readjusts his camera and gives Louisa a marker to stand on. He has me stand just off-camera for the moment.

He counts down with his fingers and Louisa starts her spiel about the holidays and last-minute shopping. Then she discusses holiday dinners and gatherings and needing the very best at the table.

At that moment, she motions me into the shot.

"We're with Gretchen Meyers of *Gretchen Meyers Bakery*, located in downtown Denver. Gretchen, you guys have been cranking out desserts and pastries all day."

I smile. "We have been. Our first customer came to pick up their order at six o'clock this morning."

She shakes her head, still smiling, of course. "Your bakery

is a local favorite, and nationwide one as well. How many orders have you shipped out?"

So, she's done some homework. This is refreshing. "All of our shipped orders were sent out earlier this week to reach tables for Christmas. We shipped out two-hundred orders."

Louisa presses a hand to her chest. "What was in those orders?"

"Everything. Breads. Cookies. Pies," I say, with pride bubbling in my voice.

"One of your most sought-after items is elegant and ornate wedding cakes." I nod at her comment. "In fact, the *Maître d' Hotel* in Aspen, who caters to an elite clientele was considering you to be their exclusive cake designer. But that honor went to your fiancé, Levi Braddock. How do you feel about that?"

Seriously? This is how I'm finding out about this? Some news gal drops this on me? Where was Levi? When did he find out? Sure, I'm happy for him, but he should have told me. He should have let me know he was chosen. I have to look like a damned fool on TV.

"Levi is the most talented cake designer I know," I say, working to keep my voice even, though I'm sure the color of my cheeks has betrayed me. "The hotel has made a fine choice in choosing him," I say with a smile.

Louisa lifts her phone. "I'm sure you've seen the cake he made that was chosen by the hotel."

As she shifts the phone in my direction, I'm sure my face has lost its composure. She is showing me a picture of my cake.

CHAPTER 16

Present

GRETCHEN

Marsha would kill me if she knew I was sitting in my bakery at ten o'clock at night, rolling out fondant.

After I left Sebastian's, I came straight back to the bakery. I slipped into my Crocs, threw an apron over my dress, and pulled back my hair. Sitting at my decorating station brings me peace, so that's why I'm here. The bowl of Halloween candy on my station threatens to make me sick, but I'm okay with that.

I have a lot of thoughts running through my head, and I'm not sure how to sort them out. So, I work.

I had always known Levi had been involved with Olive Darling. That had come up early on, after I'd met him. He didn't talk about it. In fact, I'd learned about it the same way everyone had at the culinary school, when that episode of him beating Bobby Flay appeared on TV, and Olive was there cheering him on and kissing him after.

The one time I'd asked about it, he'd brushed it off. All he had said was that it ended badly, and she didn't much like him. After that, I let that be the end of it. I didn't go searching for more information. Levi ran in circles I'd never understood until now. Now I'm sitting in my bakery thinking about the paycheck I just lost, just because of my proximity to Levi.

I let out a slow breath because I realized I was holding it in.

She saw us together, Levi and I, almost kissing—and wasn't that a bigger deal?

I put the small roller down and dust off my hands on my apron.

Picking up my coffee mug, I take a careful sip, only to realize I've been sitting there much longer than I thought. The coffee is cold.

I keep replaying what was happening when Olive came up on us. How Levi had pulled me into that hallway. How I accused him again, because I always accuse him for what he did.

But something that Levi said tonight keeps clawing at me.

Most of the problem between you and I was always assumption.

I'm guilty for immediately assuming that he did Olive wrong and that's why she hated him. Of course, I guess if she really did love that cat... but that's not my point. I've never stopped and listened to his side of the story when it comes to us.

But I caught Levi stealing ideas from me. This is different.

I pick up my detail knife and begin to carve into the fondant. I make lines, curves, circles. Each cut creates something new.

I take the pieces of fondant and mold a simple design.

I sip my cold coffee again and wince as I swallow it down.

There is no need for me to rethink what I know about Levi Braddock. I'm okay to keep on hating him—or so I keep saying to myself.

When my phone rings, I nearly fall off my stool. I'm sure it's Marsha wondering how my evening was.

I'm rather surprised to see Levi's contact come up.

Every part of me reacts differently. My brain says to let the call go through to voicemail, and then erase it. My heart says to answer it and see what he wants. My hands shake so badly that I can hardly hold my phone. My lips curl into a smile, as I think about what almost happened today.

I hate him, I kindly remind myself as I answer the phone.

"Hello."

"Gretch, can we talk?"

"We are," I say, then put him on speaker so I can continue my therapy at my design table.

"I mean face to face."

"I don't think that's a good idea. I'm going to go to bed, so—"

"I'm standing at the back door to your bakery. I see your car."

I lift my head and look at the back door, just mere feet from me. I could tell him that I'd taken an Uber home from the party. I look up. The light is on.

"Fine. I'll open the door. But I'm ready to go home. So—"

"I won't be but a minute," he promises.

What am I doing? I slip from my stool and walk to the door. I undo the top two locks before remembering to look through the hole to see if he's really outside. My luck, someone has kidnapped him and told him to call me to gain access to my bakery. It wouldn't surprise me if someone was trying to steal my ideas again and using him to do it.

Okay, I'm being silly.

I unlock the last lock and pull open the door.

Under the halo of the back light, in a heavy October mist, Levi stands there, a mask of worry on his handsome face.

"Hi," I say.

"Hi," he says. "Can I come in?"

Nodding, I step back and let him through, before engaging the locks again.

"Why are you here so late?" he asks, scanning a look over me.

I look down at my Crocs, and the dress I wore to the party, peeking out from under the apron.

"I just needed—"

"To think about what happened today?"

I shrug. "It was a big paycheck to lose, but—"

Levi steps in closer to me. "I wasn't talking about Olive Darling."

I step back, trying to convince myself that I don't know what he's talking about.

Studying his eyes, dark and settled on my face, I turn and walk back to my workstation. "I made some coffee," I say, then realize that might have already been a few hours ago.

I sit on my work stool, and Levi follows me. He looks down at the fondant on my table and smiles. "You are thinking about what happened today."

I look at all the pieces I've set out. Mistletoe. I was building mistletoe.

My eyes move back to his as he steps between me and the table. "You know what they say about mistletoe," he says, his voice low and husky.

"Levi—"

He places a finger under my chin and runs his thumb over my jaw. "We didn't finish this," he says.

"I'm not sure it's a good idea," I say, but I don't move, just as I didn't move in the hallway.

"I think it was always a good idea. We were good together once."

He presses in closer, my knees opening to allow him to

move in. Suddenly my mouth is dry, so I lick my lips, which only makes him smile more.

I should stop this. I should tell him to leave—so why can't I?

Both of his hands come to my face, and he tilts my gaze to meet his. "You can't tell me you don't want to kiss me," his voice is just a whisper.

But he's right. I can't tell him that. Instead, my body betrays me, and my hands move to his hips and pull him in.

"That's what I thought," he says before he dips his head and meets my eager mouth with his.

CHAPTER 17

Present

LEVI

Along with common sense, the air is swept out of the room as I kiss Gretchen. Memories flood back to me. The taste of her. The feel of her in my arms. The way my heart beats a different rhythm because she's always meant something to me.

From the moment I walked into that classroom, and she was sitting there ready to show off her skills, she was mine. No one else, and nothing else mattered, until we let it matter.

Her tongue sweeps through my mouth, her fingers dig into my hips, and my head spins. I have to move my hands from her face and grip her shoulders just to keep standing upright.

Our first kiss was under mistletoe. What was supposed to be a friendly peck had turned into a heated exchange of feelings we'd both had bottled up. This kiss, next to the fondant mistletoe on her worktable, feels much the same.

Gretchen pulls back briefly, perhaps to take a breath. Her eyes are wide, her lips swollen from our kisses.

"Okay, so that was unexpected," she says on a breath, her fingers still gripping me.

"Inevitable, I think." I look back at her workstation. "Mistletoe has that effect on us."

She's smiling when I look back at her. Her dark eyes are heavy with need. I can't help but move in and kiss her again.

This time, her hands come to my waist, and she begins to pull my shirt from the waistband of my pants. Her hands slide up under the fabric and touch my skin.

Every nerve in my body reacts to her touch and I pull her in closer.

"I've missed this. I've missed this so much," I say before I drown myself in another one of her kisses as her hands move over my stomach and up to my chest.

"I have too," she breathes out the words as I move my lips to her jaw, and down the side of her throat.

As I work my kisses back to her lips, I feel her pull back from me.

"What's wrong?" I ask, afraid she might actually have an answer for my question.

"It's late. I have to be back here at six. My crew starts at four, and I have to clean all of this up."

I rest my forehead to hers. "Right. I have to be at work early too," I say, realizing that for the first time in a very long time I hadn't been focused on my bakery at all.

"Do you still make those cranberry and orange muffins?" she asks as she rubs the tip of her nose against mine.

"I do."

"I miss those."

"I'll bring you one," I promise before I take an unwanted step back. "I'll help you clean this all up, and walk you to your car."

Gretchen nods as she reaches her hand into mine and links

our fingers together. "What do we do about this?" She motions between us.

"We keep doing it. We were always good at it."

She bites down on her swollen bottom lip. "You said something earlier, about the problem between us always being assumption."

I nod slowly. At least I know when I speak, she listens.

"You stole my idea and took the contract," she says, but her fingers are still linked with mine.

She doesn't believe it anymore. How could she? How could she say that and still hold on to me?

I keep my eyes on hers. "I didn't steal your idea."

She hasn't let go, but her grip has tightened. "I designed that wedding cake. The same cake you showed and took the contract."

"I was protecting you," I finally say, and then I wince at my own words.

Now she pulls her hand from mine. "Protecting me? By stealing the biggest client I was ever going to get?"

"You weren't going to get the client."

"How do you know that?"

"Because they didn't want you," I say, throwing my hands up.

The words hit her hard, and she covers her mouth with both her hands. Gretchen turns from me, but I'm not going to let this come between us again. This time she's going to hear me out.

I reach for her shoulders and turn her back to me. "Listen to me, please. Let me come clean with this once and for all."

"I don't want to hear it. I just want to go home."

"And for the first time ever, I'm going to tell you no. You're going to stay right here and talk to me."

Her eyes flash the hurt I'm causing her—again. But I need

to speak my piece. I've spent the past two years pining for her, wanting her back, only to make her hate me more. But not this time.

"Yes, the design was yours," I admit, and Gretchen's eyes go wide. "You had the better design. But I didn't take it to hurt you."

"You failed."

"I know that. Don't you think that I've spent the past two years knowing that what I did was wrong? But at the time, I felt as if I were doing it for the right reasons. That jerk at that hotel wanted your cakes. He wanted your talent, but he didn't want you."

"Well, all the more reason to steal it from me then," she shouts and walks toward her office.

I follow her. We're not done with this. Two years was too long to hold on to it, but after having had her in my arms again, I'm not going to let this go.

"I wanted him to see what he was turning down. I knew that if I could get the contract, then it would be a slap in his face to have to accept that the cake was yours."

"Your stupid idea failed, didn't it."

"Big time, but mostly because he announced it before I could tell you. That news-lady got to you before I could. It all fell apart. Gretch, don't you get it? You're the best. You're naturally gifted, and it pissed me off that he just didn't want to work with you, but he wanted your skill."

"A good fiancé would have told him where to stick it."

"And that's the point. I wasn't a good fiancé, so here we are."

Gretchen pulls her apron off over her head, causing the loosely managed bun to come free. Her curls spill over her shoulders, shadowing her dark eyes.

"I want you to go," she says.

I step closer to her. "I will. But you need to know something. You need to know that I love you, and I've never stopped loving you."

"That's a funny thing to say when you had a date tonight."

"Yeah, well, as I can't even think of her name, I'm not too worried about that. What I'm worried about is you."

"Oh, you should have stopped worrying about me years ago."

I shake my head. "I worry that you'll never see me the same."

"You're right. You're deceiving."

"And you're unwilling to bend," I counter.

"I don't see why I should."

"You shouldn't," I say, and the confusion that masks her face is clear. "You never should bend, but you should stop for a second and listen once in a while. Had you let me explain myself two years ago, maybe..."

I rake my fingers through my hair to gain my composure back. I don't want to walk out of that bakery without the promise that she'll be back in my arms.

When I look back at her, there are tears in her eyes. "I didn't let you explain."

"No."

"I left."

"Yes," I say, and I watch it wash over her, sink in, make its mark.

Gretchen pulls her purse out of the bottom drawer of her desk and slips it over her shoulder. Moving past me, she takes her coat off the hook, and fumbles to get her arms in it.

"Are you coming?" she asks, nearly frantic.

"Where am I going?"

Gretchen stops fighting the coat and looks at me with only

one arm through. Her hair is wild, and her eyes are laser-focused on me.

"Home with me."

And with that, she turns and walks out of the office.

CHAPTER 18

Present

LEVI

There are murmurs when I walk through the front door of *Gretchen Meyers Bakery* with a cake box in hand. Marsha looks up from a cake she's decorating, and quickly puts the frosting bag down. Moving to intercept me, she blocks my path to Gretchen's door.

"What are you doing here?" she asks in a hushed tone.

"I'm here to see Gretchen."

"I think you should go."

I would have thought they spoke more than they obviously do. Or Gretchen would have said something to her about the reason she was so tired this morning. Neither of us could get out of bed—or wanted to. Aerial had seen right through me; I would have thought Marsha would have figured it out too.

I open the box to show her the orange and cranberry muffins, assuming she'll understand the meaning.

Marsha lifts her eyes to meet mine. "Are you trying to bribe her?"

"Why would I do that? Hasn't she told you? We're together again," I whisper.

By the crease deepening between her brows, they have not had this conversation.

A moment later, Gretchen's office door flies open, and she stands there with her hands on her hips and a look burning into me so fiery it would melt the frosting off a cake.

"Get in here," she growls as she points to me.

I exchange a glance with Marsha. Was this what she was warning me about?

I close the muffin box and walk into the office. I hear the door slam behind me and lock.

"You did it again! I let you back into my life for a mere few hours and you do it to me again!" She's shouting, not worried about the people gathering outside the door to listen—whom I can see on the monitor doing just that.

I set down the box on her desk. "I'm going to need some clarification."

"Oh, you're smooth, aren't you?" She presses her hands to her face. "I'm so stupid."

I hold my hands up in surrender, though I'm not guilty of anything this time. "Take a breath and tell me what's going on."

"Why did you come here last night?"

"To talk to you."

"You came here to steal from me, to take my ideas," she lets out a muffled scream. "And I took you home. I'm so stupid."

Now I step to her. "I didn't steal anything. I don't know what you're talking about."

"Hermon's of Denver Hotel."

"We're competing for their Christmas display."

"And you sold me out! You gave her my cake design."

This time I reach for Gretchen and pull her toward me so that she's standing toe to toe with me. "Are you kidding me? You think I'd do that?"

"You stole from me before," she argues.

"And I explained myself. Right or wrong, I did that with you in mind. But this..." I draw back and rub my tired eyes. "This, I didn't do."

Gretchen moves behind her desk and turns her computer screen so that I can see it.

"Who sent this to you?" I ask, looking at the screen.

"mystic199," she says. "I don't know who that is. All I know is this is Charlotte's bakery, and that is my design." She points to the reindeer with the bright nose.

"Yeah, well that's mine," I say, pointing to the sparkly snowman.

Gretchen studies the cake I've pointed to. "Really? A snowman?"

I drop my shoulders. "Really? A reindeer?" I mimic her.

She puckers her lips. "What do we do?"

I shake my head. "We can turn her in, but we don't know that that's her design. Maybe she's toying with us." I press my fingers to my temples. "We could back out," I suggest, but it's met with furious eyes.

"I've worked for months to get that cake just right. I know hers is smaller, mine is life-sized."

I chuckle. "You have a life-sized reindeer taking up space in your cooler?"

"And I know you have some snowman in yours."

She was right. I do.

I watched Gretchen pace a small circle in her office, tapping her fingers to her lips. "We only have three weeks to create something new," she ponders.

"I say we go down there and confront her."

Gretchen shakes her head. "No, we beat her." She lifts her eyes to meet mine. "She's stealing our ideas because she doesn't have any of her own. I've beaten her out of every contract and every contest since she fired me. And, if I didn't win it, you did."

I wait for her to throw in *at any cost*, but she's not. Her brain is turning, and ideas are popping. I've seen this before. This is part of her process.

"I need a partner," she says, turning to look at me.

"We are partners," I say taking a step toward her. "I think we officially decided that last night."

She shakes her head. "No. That'll just get in the way."

I want to argue, but she's not even focused on me now. "Okay, a partner for what?"

She lifts her eyes again and they lock onto me. "We're going to beat her—together."

"Keep talking."

"We're going to create something that will make people forget she exists." Her hands are up in her hair. "Two feuding bakeries that team up to take the other down. We won't point fingers. We won't shout that she's a traitor. We'll win this thing with our talents. Imagine the publicity we could get when we win. You're already a household name nationwide. Us winning this will take away any limelight she thinks she'll have."

Her plan sounds vindictive in its delivery, but she's focused on winning with talent.

"What do you think?" she asks, and I smile.

"I think I love you."

Her face loses the joyful expression that had masked the anger from when I'd walked in. Now disappointment creases her eyes and turns down her mouth.

"No. What happened yesterday, that was—"

"Wonderful."

"Levi, we can't do that again. We can't get mixed up with each other."

"We've always been mixed up with each other."

She draws in a breath. "And it's hurtful. We need to go into this as partners for this cause. We can do this. No one is more talented than you and me, and together we're unstoppable. But we can't do this if we're starry-eyed."

I think she's wrong. I don't want to step back from what happened last night. I don't want to forget it all. I also don't want to lose any time I get to have with her.

"If you think that's best," I say.

"I do. So will you partner with me on this?"

I want to draw her into my arms and kiss her mouth to give her my answer. I want to tell her again that I love her, and I support any ideas she might have.

Instead, I hold out my hand to her. "I'll be your partner," I say.

Gretchen takes my hand and shakes it. "Then let's hash out a plan."

CHAPTER 19

Present

GRETCHEN

Sure, this is our busiest time of the season. Thanksgiving is only two weeks away and the orders are pouring in. Christmas orders will be right on the heels of Thanksgiving.

But Marsha is taking the lead on everything in the bakery. And, as much as it hurts me to say it, Aerial is doing the same for Levi. She's loyal, hardworking, and an asset to him.

After someone sold us out, presumably someone with access to our staff—or sadly multiple people on our staffs—we agreed to rent a kitchen for the next few weeks to work on our project in private.

The door opens to the rented kitchen just after seven o'clock in the evening, and Levi strolls through with takeout.

There are dark circles under his eyes, and his hair is just long enough to pull back now into a small ponytail. I wonder if he'll cut it or leave it.

"I know we had Chinese the other night but—"

"It'll be perfect. Thank you," I say as he sets it down on the table. "Everything all right?"

He nods and begins to unpack the bags.

We put together something new, and I think it's going to be miraculous and modern.

Our cake design is an elf, laying on his stomach, his feet crossed at his ankles, and his fists under his chin gleefully watching Santa's journey on a tablet. The drawing is adorable. Sculpting him has been challenging, but not out of our realm. We have one week before the cakes are displayed for voting.

But working with Levi so closely and not acknowledging that spark between us, it's harder than I thought it would be. I didn't realize just how much I'd missed him until we had our one night together, and then I established a new set of rules.

Maybe we can see how this turns out.

"Is the Christmas music for inspiration?" he asks as he sits down at the table where we have all our notes and drawings. He pulls out a crab cheese Rangoon and hands it to me. He knows I crave these things.

"Thank you," I say, taking the Rangoon from him. "And yes. The air is changing. We're supposed to get a dusting of snow this week, and I'm ready for some holiday cheer."

"That would be nice, wouldn't it?"

"I forget each year just how busy it gets," I admit as I bite into the deep-fried puff. "I sometimes feel as if we miss out on all the merriment of the holidays."

He nods. "You're right. We do."

He's deep in thought, I can tell. He's eating, but he's not tasting. He's talking, but only in answers to my own thoughts.

"What's on your mind?" I ask and Levi lifts his eyes to meet mine.

"Just normal—"

"No. This isn't normal," I say, reaching my hand across the table and covering his.

He looks down to where our hands are, turns his so that our palms touch, and links our fingers.

"You know what we haven't done in years?"

I shake my head. "What?"

"Dance," he says as he stands and pulls me to my feet.

"We should—"

"Dance," he says again, easing me against him while the speakers play *White Christmas*.

I lean into him, my head to his chest, his arms wrapped around me. The tension in my muscles melts away, and his heartbeat slows under my ear. He needed this. I needed this.

"We're close to having this all—"

"Shh," his breath is in my ear. "Just a few more moments."

This was why I said we couldn't do this project if we were involved. We're wasting time dancing, holding, breathing in one another.

When the song finished, and *Grandma Got Ran Over by a Reindeer* began to play, we both laughed and eased apart.

"Thank you," he says. "I needed that."

"Hard day?"

He nods. "You could say that. Let's get this guy going. We should have him done in two days."

"Just in time."

Our elf is perfect, and my stomach is fluttering watching him be loaded into the van. I've never—ever—been prouder of a cake. And the fact that Levi and I created him together brings me so much joy.

As the doors to the van are closed, and it pulls away, I'm a little weepy. It's as if my child were going to school without saying goodbye to me.

"Well, that's it," Levi says. "All that's left is for you to show up and claim your prize."

I turn my head to look up at him. "Me? You mean we."

Levi turns me to face him, pulling me in. As his arms wrap around me, I decide this intimate moment has been earned, and I wrap my arms around him.

"I mean you," he says again. "I stepped out of the competition. This is yours to win. You deserve it."

"But we—"

"Are a great team," he says. "But this isn't the team I want to be on. Not your cake team."

Levi brushes a strand of hair from my forehead.

"The past few weeks have done a lot for my soul. You being here with me, it makes me remember what's important, and that's you."

"But, Levi—"

"Go. Your cake is on its way to greatness. You're going to be inundated with TV interviews and press. After this, you'll be the most sought-after cake designer in the world."

My lip trembles. But we're a team. He has to be there with me. I didn't do this alone. I don't want to be alone.

And that's when it hits me. I do still love this man, and I want to be with him—a team.

Levi releases me, slips on his coat and gloves, and walks to the door.

"Levi—"

He turns, shaking his head. "I'll watch for you. You're going to do great things."

CHAPTER 20

Present

GRETCHEN

The atrium of the hotel is decorated for the holidays, and in the center is the gingerbread Santa's Workshop, and it's as glorious as I'd imagined it would be.

The cakes are displayed—ours and Charlotte's.

I'm sure I'm going to be sick. There are hundreds of people circling the display. My entire team is there to cheer me on, and Levi's team is there as well. But Levi is nowhere.

Charlotte's cake is a reindeer pulling a sled with a snow-man, but her design looks exactly like mine. And the snow-man, looks just like the drawings and pictures that Levi showed me of his design.

As the ceremony begins, I scan the crowd looking for Levi. I really thought he'd be here. He'd taken his name off the cake and pulled his entry, but I feel wrong doing this without him. We were a team.

"Guess he couldn't handle it, huh?" Charlotte says through her grin.

"He doesn't need it."

"We all need this kind of publicity. I mean, he's not as hot as he was, or thinks he is."

I'm ready to go at it, an all-out cat fight on national TV if I have to, but my thoughts are interrupted as one of the men in charge of the competition leans in to Charlotte and whispers in her ear.

Her eyes go wide, and she looks in my direction. I have no idea what's going on, but she's escorted away without another word.

I look toward Marsha who is standing with our team smiling up at me.

The crew who organized the display moves in around Charlotte's cake, and the table on which her cake is displayed, is rolled out of the atrium, and my cake—our cake—is rolled to the center.

I turn toward the emcee. "What's going on?"

"I'm not quite sure. Judging hasn't finished yet," he says.

Charlotte's staff begins to disperse, and now Marsha and Aerial are standing shoulder to shoulder looking in my direction.

"It appears that *Charlotte's Goodies* has been removed from the competition," the emcee says quietly to me.

"Removed?"

"There is word that she attempted to bribe one of the judges and might have lifted other competitor's plans to compete this year."

I turn my attention back to Marsha and Aerial. They're both smiling up at me. What hand did they have in this, I wonder.

"What does that mean?" I ask the emcee.

"It appears that with Mr. Braddock withdrawing, then you are the winner."

I wrinkle my nose. "Just like that?"

"Well," he looks at his notes. "Yes."

I honestly thought the win would feel better. Sure, maybe Charlotte got what she deserved, but Levi should be standing there with me. Maybe I should resign from the competition too. It's not fair that—

I can't even finish my thought before the emcee makes the announcement that *Gretchen Meyers Bakery* has won the competition.

My team cheers.

Levi's team cheers.

There is champagne opened. I'm handed an enormous check, and photos are taken. The emcee hands me the keys to the sprinter van.

From that moment on I'm in the spotlight. I'm on display.

I can hardly remember Thanksgiving. It was a whirlwind of orders going out the door and special appearances on local TV.

Shortly after that, Marsha and I are on a flight to New York to do a segment on the Today show.

The dream to see New York at Christmas is checked off my bucket list, as is an appearance on the Today show, and being a guest chef at a high-end restaurant that was serving my desserts.

But the whole while, I think about how I'd rather be doing these things with Levi.

"What are you thinking?" Marsha nudges me on our flight back to Colorado.

"This still feels wrong to me," I say, noticing that Marsha's showing me the screen on her phone, and a publisher has reached out about doing a cookbook with me.

I pull the phone from her hand and read the email. Then I

exchange glances with her. Mine has to show confusion, but hers is pure joy.

"I can't do all of this," I say.

"You're already doing all of this," she defends. "Enjoy this."

"I didn't make that cake on my own."

"No one cares."

"I care," I say.

Marsha takes my hand in hers. "He did it because he loves you, and you deserve all of this."

"He feels as if he owes it to me."

"He does," she confirms, and shifts in her seat. "Aerial says he's happy for you. And so proud."

"And what part in all of this did you and Aerial have?"

Her grin widens as she sits back in her seat and tucks her phone into the pocket in the seat in front of her.

"She found out the snitch was a delivery driver. We have a friend or two who were working with Charlotte, and they were looking for new jobs. They got us the proof that she'd stolen your designs, and we turned them over. The hotel was none too pleased," she says.

"I won by default."

"You won with the best cake," she reminds me.

"He should have been there."

"So, what do you do?"

Looking out over the snowy scenery outside the plane, I contemplate my next move.

Sliding on my headphones, I hit play on my music and *White Christmas* plays in my ears.

Smiling to myself, I say, "I think I know exactly what I'm going to do."

Other Titles from

5 PRINCE PUBLISHING

5PrinceBooks.com
Composing Laney *S.E. Reichert*
Heartfire *Jessica Mehring*
Vampires of Atlantis *Courtney Davis*
Liz's Roadtrip *Bernadette Marie*
Back to the 80s *S.E. Reichert & Kerrie Flanagan*
Granting Katelyn *S.E. Reichert*
Ghosts of Alda *Russell Archey*
The Serpent and the Firefly *Courtney Davis*
Raising Elle *S.E. Reichert*
Rom Com Movie Club No.3 *Bernadette Marie*
Rom Com Movie Club No.2 *Bernadette Marie*
Rom Com Movie Club No.1 *Bernadette Marie*
A Crossbow Christmas *Ann Swann*
Hot For Teacher *Felicia Carparelli*
The Happily Ever After Bookstore *Bernadette Marie*
Perfect Mrs Claus *Barbara Matteson*
Princess of Prias *Courtney Davis*
Paige and the Reluctant Artist *Darci Garcia*
A Spider in the Garden *Courtney Davis*

Epilogue

PRESENT

GRETCHEN

Christmas morning, and for the first time since I was a child, I feel the Christmas energy buzzing in the air.

I couldn't sleep last night. It was as if Santa Claus was expected to show up at my house at any moment.

My tree is only half-decorated—or was. I took all of the ornaments off it last night and put them in a box by the door. I have enough mistletoe for every doorway in Denver in another box.

I load all the boxes into my car and drive over to Levi's.

I'm not sure how it happened, but I find a parking spot, right in front of Levi's building. I haul the boxes up three flights of stairs and quietly set them on the ground.

With a roll of tape in one hand, I pull mistletoe out of a box and begin to outline the doorframe with it. When he opens his door, he'll have to kiss me. That was the rule. Mistletoe could never be passed up.

When the doorframe is sufficiently covered, I knock.

Tap! Tap, tap-tap! Pause. *Tap! Tap, tap-tap!*

Picking up the ornament box, I wait for him to answer, but he never does.

I knock again, and then begin to worry. Maybe he's inside but he isn't alone. Maybe he left town. Maybe he's just gone.

As I lift my hand to knock again, his voice comes from behind me.

"That's an awful lot of mistletoe."

I turn, nearly dropping the box of ornaments. "You're not here. I mean you are, but you're not home."

"I was trying to find some Christmas cheer. It looks like I found it," he says looking at the decor around his door.

"I hope you don't mind that I—"

"I don't mind at all," he says. His eyes take in the entire sight of me, and he smiles. "In fact, I just left your bakery."

I narrow my gaze on him. "We're not open."

"I know. Sometimes when I miss you, I stand and look at your window display."

I open my mouth to speak, but I don't know what to say.

Levi steps in closer. "Don't be mad, but I've done it for years. Sometimes, I can see you in the back working on special projects."

"You've spied on me?"

"I've admired you working," he corrects. Looking down into the box in my hands, he lets out a small laugh. "What is all of this?"

"Christmas tree ornaments. I didn't even finish decorating my tree, I've been so busy."

"You looked beautiful on TV," he says.

"You watched me?"

"Of course I did. You were shining. How could I miss it?"

I pucker my lips because tears are burning behind my eyes, and if I don't control it, I'm going to cry. "You should have been by my side," I said.

"I was. Trust me, I was."

"That cake was ours."

Levi nods, brushing back a stray hair from my face, as he always does. "It was. So let me use the van for deliveries too," he says, and now I laugh, but not before the tears break free.

"I love you," I blurt out the words. "I don't want to ever compete against you again."

Levi takes the box from my hands. "Never?"

"No. A client is one thing. But things like contracts and hotels, we should have always been doing that together."

He nods slowly. "Come inside. Let's put these ornaments on the tree."

I turn back and look at the door. "I don't think we can just walk in," I say.

He considers my statement. Pulling the keys from his pocket, he slides them into the lock, and pushes the door open. Setting the box just inside his apartment, he turns back to me.

Raising his hands to cup my face, his eyes search mine. "That first time I kissed you under the mistletoe, I thought it was just going to be a friendly kiss. I had no idea the sparks that were set off that night were buried so deep," he says. "That moment, in Charlotte's doorway, I fell in love with you deeper than I already was as your friend."

"Really?"

"Really."

Levi dips his head and brushes his lips over mine. "I want to be the only man you ever kiss under mistletoe."

With that, he pulls me to him, his mouth opening to mine. My tongue sweeps out and is met by his. Those sparks are still there. We've shared thousands of kisses, but this one, it's like the first—a new start.

As our mouths work together, Levi manages to turn me

into his apartment, shutting the door behind me, and pushing me up against it.

"I love you, Gretchen. I love everything about you."

"I love you too." I say, reaching my hands up into his hair to realize he's cut it off again. I laugh against his lips. "Merry Christmas."

"It sure is," he says before kissing me again.

Heat resonates through me as he pulls me against him tightly, our coats still clinging to us, the darkness of the apartment enveloping us.

As we pull apart, he rests his forehead to mine. "Years ago, when you walked out of our place, you didn't take your Christmas present."

I lift a brow. "I didn't?"

"It was in the tree."

I clamp my lips between my teeth. "I remember seeing it."

"I knew you had." He gently kisses my lips. "It's still there, waiting for you."

"That was years ago."

"Might have been. But it's still there."

Levi drops his arms to his side and stands back, an invitation for me to go toward the tree.

His tree isn't any more decorated than mine had been. I laugh when I notice the mistletoe at the top, just as we'd done all those years ago.

He nods, encouraging me to look for the box.

It was small, I remember, and not under the tree but in the tree.

When I find it, my fingers begin to tingle, and I have to remember to breathe.

I remove it from the branch and sit with it in my hands, just looking at the box.

"Open it," he says, his voice is right behind me now.

I lift the lid to expose a ring, the diamond in the shape of a snowflake.

"Every person has a talent, much like a snowflake, they are alike, but never the same." He quotes what I told him when we met.

"Levi—"

He takes the ring from the box. "The ring, and I, have been waiting years for you. We'd love to have you back forever," he says, holding the ring poised at my finger.

"I'll stay forever," I promise.

"Will you marry me?"

"Of course I will."

Smiling, he slides the ring on my finger. "There's mistletoe on the top of this tree," he says.

"I saw that."

"You know what it means if there's mistletoe?"

"I do. It means that every good memory I have, started as a moment under the mistletoe."

About the Author

Bestselling Author Bernadette Marie writes contemporary romances and believes in Happily Ever After. The married mother of five believes in love at first sight, quick love, and second chances. An avid martial artist, Bernadette Marie is a certified instructor and holds a second degree black belt in Tang Soo Do. She loves Tai Chi, traveling to Disney parks, and having lunch with friends. When not writing, or running her own publishing house, Bernadette is probably immersed in a Rom Com, from which she will often quote one liners.